THE **JOURNEY** PRIZE

STORIES

WINNERS OF THE $10,000 JOURNEY PRIZE

1989
Holley Rubinsky for
"Rapid Transits"

1990
Cynthia Flood for "My Father
Took a Cake to France"

1991
Yann Martel for "The Facts
Behind the Helsinki Roccamatios"

1992
Rozena Maart for "No Rosa,
No District Six"

1993
Gayla Reid for
"Sister Doyle's Men"

1994
Melissa Hardy for
"Long Man the River"

1995
Kathryn Woodward for "Of
Marranos and Gilded Angels"

1996
Elyse Gasco for "Can You Wave
Bye Bye, Baby?"

1997 (shared)
Gabriella Goliger for
"Maladies of the Inner Ear"

Anne Simpson for
"Dreaming Snow"

1998
John Brooke for
"The Finer Points of Apples"

1999
Alissa York for "The Back of the
Bear's Mouth"

2000
Timothy Taylor for
"Doves of Townsend"

2001
Kevin Armstrong for
"The Cane Field"

2002
Jocelyn Brown for "Miss Canada"

2003
Jessica Grant for
"My Husband's Jump"

2004
Devin Krukoff for
"The Last Spark"

2005
Matt Shaw for "Matchbook for a
Mother's Hair"

2006
Heather Birrell for
"BriannaSusannaAlana"

THE BEST OF CANADA'S NEW WRITERS

THE **JOURNEY** PRIZE

STORIES

SELECTED BY
CAROLINE **ADDERSON**
DAVID **BEZMOZGIS**
DIONNE **BRAND**

McCLELLAND & STEWART

Library and Archives Canada has catalogued this publication as follows:

A CIP catalogue record for this book is available from Library and Archives Canada

ISBN 978-0-7710-9561-0

We acknowledge the financial support of the Government of Canada through the Book Publishing Industry Development Program and that of the Government of Ontario through the Ontario Media Development Corporation's Ontario Book Initiative. We further acknowledge the support of the Canada Council for the Arts and the Ontario Arts Council for our publishing program.

"Twelve Versions of Lech" © Andrew J. Borkowski; "OZY" © Craig Boyko;
"The Curve of the Earth" © Grant Buday; "High-water Mark" © Nicole Dixon;
"Swimming in Zanzibar" © Krista Foss; "Respite" © Pasha Malla;
"After Summer" © Alice Petersen; "My Hungarian Sister" © Patricia Robertson;
"Chilly Girl" © Rebecca Rosenblum; "How Eunice Got Her Baby" © Nicholas Ruddock;
"Stardust" © Jean Van Loon.
These stories are reprinted with permission of the authors.

Typeset in Janson by M&S, Toronto
Printed and bound in Canada

 ANCIENT FOREST
FRIENDLY

McClelland & Stewart Ltd.
75 Sherbourne Street
Toronto, Ontario
M5A 2P9
www.mcclelland.com

1 2 3 4 5   11 10 09 08 07

The $10,000 Journey Prize is awarded annually to a new and developing writer of distinction. This award, now in its nineteenth year, and given for the seventh time in association with the Writers' Trust of Canada as the Writers' Trust of Canada/ McClelland & Stewart Journey Prize, is made possible by James A. Michener's generous donation of his Canadian royalty earnings from his novel *Journey*, published by McClelland & Stewart in 1988. The Journey Prize itself is the most significant monetary award given in Canada to a writer at the beginning of his or her career for a short story or excerpt from a fiction work in progress. The winner of this year's Journey Prize will be selected from among the eleven stories in this book.

The Journey Prize Stories has established itself as the most prestigious annual fiction anthology in the country, introducing readers to the finest new writers from coast to coast for almost two decades. It has become a who's who of up-and-coming writers, and many of the authors whose early work has appeared in the anthology's pages have gone on to distinguish themselves with collections of short stories, novels, and literary awards. The anthology comprises a selection from submissions made by the editors of literary journals from across the country, who have chosen what, in their view, is the most exciting writing in English that they have published in the previous year. In recognition of the vital role journals play in discovering new writers, McClelland & Stewart makes its own award of $2,000 to the journal that originally published and submitted the winning entry.

This year the selection jury, comprising multi-award-winning writers Caroline Adderson, David Bezmozgis, and Dionne Brand, read a total of seventy-six submissions without knowing the names of the authors or those of the journals in which the stories had originally appeared. McClelland & Stewart would like to thank the jury for their efforts in selecting this year's anthology and, ultimately, the winner of this year's Journey Prize.

McClelland & Stewart would also like to acknowledge the continuing enthusiastic support of writers, literary journal editors, and the public in the common celebration of the emergence of new voices in Canadian fiction.

For more information about *The Journey Prize Stories*, please consult our website: www.mcclelland.com/jps.

CONTENTS

CAROLINE ADDERSON

I've had easier jobs. I once deejayed on a community radio station in a language I could barely speak. Another time I helped shingle a roof badly. For this gig I read some of the seventy-six stories nominated for this year's Journey Prize twice, at least a dozen stories three times, and a few even four times. Every word. Then I had to choose which ones I liked best when, really, I would rather have mailed out medals to all seventy-six writers for actually caring about literature. But the job was to choose, so I did.

At this stage in my reading and writing life, I'm no longer as interested in technical perfection as I am in innovation. At the very least I want to be surprised, or delighted, or moved; a blessing on the writer who does all three. And *puh-lease*, a little wit. For these reasons "Twelve Versions of Lech" jumped right out at me. Andrew J. Borkowski dispenses entirely with the traditional linear narrative yet still manages to make me feel for his awed narrator and the enigmatic Lech. Character *is* the story and wit abounds. Pasha Malla's "Respite" worked just as well. The plight of Womack as a novelist and boyfriend was both funny and maddening, and the image of the dying boy – who communicates more with his moans than Womack does in all his word-processing – as he's dragged around the house by Womack, broke my heart. And I loved Nicole Dixon's "High-water Mark" for how the smart-ass narrator single-handedly saves the story from melodrama with the power of her voice. Cancer, dead dads, dead babies – and I laughed? That's some feat.

A huge congratulations to all the writers whose work appears in these pages.

CAROLINE ADDERSON is the author of two internationally published novels, *A History of Forgetting* and *Sitting Practice*, and two collections of short stories, *Bad Imaginings* and *Pleased to Meet You*. Her work has won her two Ethel Wilson Fiction Prizes, three CBC Literary Awards, as well as numerous nominations, including for the Scotiabank Giller Prize longlist, the Governor General's Literary Award, the Rogers Writers' Trust Fiction Prize, and the Commonwealth Writers' Prize. Adderson is the recipient of the 2006 Marian Engel Award, given to an outstanding female writer in mid-career.

DAVID BEZMOZGIS

What kind of story belongs in a volume entitled *The Journey Prize Stories*? This was the question I put to myself when I sat down to read the seventy-six stories submitted for consideration. I could conceive of several approaches but I ultimately settled on the simplest one. I looked for the stories that seemed to be the most accomplished, in which the authors had best met the difficult challenge of matching language to feeling. I was pleased to find a number of such stories, some of them quite exceptional, truly among the best I'd read in recent memory.

The seventy-six stories we jurors received were organized alphabetically, and so it wasn't long before I encountered

Alice Petersen's lovely story, "After Summer." In only three evocative pages, Petersen sketches a portrait of a girl's fond recollections of summers spent at a boathouse in the Laurentians with her father and brother. The father is a mailman and aspiring poet who devotes many of those summer afternoons to "typing up the poems he carried in his head during the rest of the year." These summers are an idyll that comes to an end when the father meets a woman who cares little for poetry or rustic living. To please the woman, the father becomes a dry-cleaner and settles down to a more conventional life. Everything changes. The narrator's brother moves away and ends up as a handyman on a home renovating show. The narrator relates all of this breezily and empathetically. About her brother, the narrator wryly observes: "The dentist always said that Jake had too many teeth, but he had enough for television." She wishes things would go back to the way they were, but understands that they won't. The story is balanced between this sense of nostalgia and acceptance, and sustained by the narrator's charming voice and her gift for physical description. We are given: "the edgy smell" of bats, "the hiss and judder" of a compressor, and "the punking noise" dry-cleaning receipts make when impaled on their spike.

Darker, but also imbued with a charming, sing-song voice, is Nicholas Ruddock's "How Eunice Got Her Baby." Though the title suggests that the story will feature Eunice, it instead features Eunice's freewheeling older sister, Florence, the mother of the baby in question. How Eunice ends up getting Florence's baby is ultimately tragic – "there's not too many good ways you can inherit a baby," Eunice says – and yet Ruddock reveals the full extent of the tragedy only at the very end. Until then, he spins a lively tale of the ill-fated romance between Florence and a man who is described as having "the spirit of a criminal born." Set in Newfoundland, the story is buoyed by the local rhythms of speech and thought. Ruddock has a refined ear for dialogue and a mischievous sense of humour. He also knows how to bring a story to a memorable conclusion.

Craig Boyko's "OZY" begins and ends with a curious column of numbers and letters. These, we learn, represent the high scores for a video game called *Ballistic Obliteration*. If this sounds like a puerile or questionable idea for a story, it is all the more to Boyko's credit that he makes this material transcend every expectation, and elevates it to the status of true art. The story Boyko gives us is funny, bittersweet, and very moving. With great skill and economy, he presents a large ensemble cast and gives each character a role in his idiosyncratic and uncommonly suspenseful narrative. Using the video game as a point of departure, Boyko somehow manages to capture, celebrate, and mourn the passing of childhood and also to reflect upon the enigma of mortality. "I was good at something once," the eponymous OZY remarks near the end of the story. "Great, even. It was a long time ago. I was ten. Now I'm forty-three and not good at much of anything. I'm not complaining. You're only forty-three and not good at anything for a short time. But you will have once been ten and good at something forever." The wisdom of this sentiment is stirring and irrefutable, and it is representative of the high level of emotion and craft Boyko achieves throughout the story.

These and the other 2007 Journey Prize stories testify to the considerable talent of the selected writers and to the healthy state of the short story form in Canada. I am honoured to have had the opportunity to read their work and to have discussed it with my fellow jurors, Caroline Adderson and Dionne Brand. I also commend McClelland & Stewart for their enthusiasm for and commitment to this series, as well as the editors of the magazines and journals in which these stories originally appeared.

DAVID BEZMOZGIS's writing has appeared in magazines such as *Harper's*, *The New Yorker*, and *The Walrus*, and has been anthologized in *Best American Short Stories, 2005* and *2006*. His first book of fiction, *Natasha and Other Stories*, was published to wide critical acclaim and won several awards, including a regional Commonwealth Writers' Prize for Best First Book, the Canadian Jewish Book Award for Fiction, and the Danuta Gleed Literary Award. David Bezmozgis lives in Toronto.

DIONNE BRAND

A media of banal reality television, repetitive police and hospital dramas, half-hourly regurgitations of old "news," blockbuster schlock films, and the dross of internet information daily challenge the short story and the novel for position in making meaning of the everyday. Poets have already moved, or have been carried away, to another planet, but novelists and short story writers are possibly more implicated in the battle over narration. And short story writers are perhaps the guerrillas of them all, staging elegant pinpoint attacks and constant mysterious raids on the terrain of meaning. (So hard to resist the war rhetoric that's become the dominant discourse of our time.) Still, there is so much work that today's short story must do, and do in the face of intense pressure. First, there are its own internal purposes, particular and solitary, as well as shouldering the work of defying the new sickly regimes of narration. A short story today, it seems to me, has to summon the unused and ignored capacities for thought and emotion which mass media finds inefficient. To use an idea from the French philosopher Baudrillard, the short story must disrupt the circuitry of the hyperreal. All this pressure of course belies the form's modesty, but then again perhaps that very modesty is its strength and how the short story does what it does; how it confronts the busy, noisy circuitry of post-modern informational debris.

The stories in this volume are certainly in lively conversation with the hyperreal. Presumed affinities fail, and new affinities are realized, in "Swimming to Zanzibar," the evocatively drawn story by Krista Foss. In the story, the central character, Regina, travels to Zanzibar trying to find something outside of herself and ends up, perhaps, finding herself. "Chilly Girl" by Rebecca Rosenblum is cunning and seamless in its attention to language. It is an otherworldly postmodern fable, a glass-delicate fairy tale. There isn't a wasted word here and all the words are surprising in their reconstruction of reality. Grant Buday's "The Curve of the Earth" follows the unexpected geographic and emotional arc of its protagonist's life: Canada, Venice, Romania; flight, return, recognition, and flight. In this highly polished story, Buday navigates the indistinct materials of family.

These are only a few of the stories to be found in this volume, stories which my co-jurors and I felt broke the surface of the information overload and forestalled the frequent and futile post-mortems for the short story.

DIONNE BRAND is a multi-award-winning poet, essayist, and novelist living in Toronto. Her nine volumes of poetry include *Land to Light On*, *thirsty*, and *Inventory*. Her most recent novel, *What We All Long For*, was published to great acclaim in Canada and Italy in 2005, and won the Toronto Book Award. In 2006, she won the Harbourfront Festival Prize for her contribution to the world of books and writing. In addition to her literary accomplishments, Brand is Professor of English in the School of English and Theatre Studies at the University of Guelph.

THE **JOURNEY** PRIZE

STORIES

KRISTA FOSS

SWIMMING IN ZANZIBAR

"Bububu."

Regina read aloud the sign.

"Bububu," she said again, as if the Swahili was a bit of butter smeared on her lips.

"Hmm?" said the Brit filmmaker, but he was not really interested.

The clouds, dark violets, pressed inward.

The other three dozed as the taxi bumped and rattled over the potholes left by a month of rains. A fine resin of sweat formed on her brow, made her back damp. Regina was the only one who wanted to swim. She'd insisted, a bit shrilly she'd admit, that they travel to the beach before they left Zanzibar. So there was no time to stop in Bububu, to see if it lived up to its name. Another corner of Africa seen through a moving window. She bit the bottom of her lip.

"Why?" the Brit had asked slightly irritated, "Is it so damn important to swim?"

"It just is," was all she could say. "It may be the only time I see the Indian Ocean."

She didn't tell him she needed to wash the last three weeks from her body, its heavy grit of disappointment. He'd insisted on coming anyway, the one free afternoon in Zanzibar they could have spent apart.

The Brit drummed his fingers on the edge of the backseat window.

He asked for the time. He sighed.

The detour to the ocean was taking longer than he expected, than she expected too. Perhaps he would say something, demand the taxi head back to the Stone Town, so he could salvage the few hours they had left on the island.

The darkening clouds were making things worse. What if the others woke up now and second-guessed the effort? she worried. It was rainy season in Zanzibar. A swim was hardly a sure thing.

The three weeks, four countries, eleven flights, were supposed to have been a career-making adventure – this trip across the world to assist a fellow documentary maker whose work she admired, hoped to emulate. She had opted out of another project for it. She had stiffed people, pissed them off. But she would help bring the world's attention to a neglected issue and great suffering. She was going to make a difference. Making a few people at home angry was a small price to pay.

They'd met for the first time in a Schipol departure lounge.

"We really don't read much about Canada in our newspapers," the Brit remarked to her soon after shaking her hand. "Does anything go on there worth caring about?"

She'd let out an involuntary laugh.

I am trying to like you, you prick, she thought.

She'd stuffed her pockets with Droste pastilles for the trip. Now a mouthful of Dutch chocolate would remind her of the sting of burning wood in the Kampala night; the school children pressing their faces against the windows to beg for the rich strangers' empty water bottles; frangipani and bougainvillea splashing grass huts with cartoon colours along bumpy Ugandan roads.

The taste had bitter notes too.

"Gina-r!" he'd barked at her, truncating and mangling her name in a double insult.

"Get the bloody camera over here . . . we're missing the shot! Puhleese."

In Jinja, he'd simply grabbed the back-up Super 8 from her with a harrumph. She blushed in the hot African sun, while the official from the Ugandan Ministry of Communication shifted nervously and loosened his tie.

At other times, his contempt was more civil. But it was contempt nonetheless. She caught him rolling his eyes at her incessant borrowing of guidebooks, her constant naming of things, her gasp of delight when they drove by olive baboons near the border with Kenya. What kind of tree is that? Is that a marabou nest? Roll. Sigh.

Now that it was nearly over, she had only the Indian Ocean as succour. They bumped and jogged across the ninety-square-kilometre island. They were tired and tired of each other. And she, who'd insisted on swimming, had taken them all farther from the old Stone Town, with its white edifices fil-igreed with mildew and its aristocratic East Indian hoteliers, keepers of air conditioning, Internet, and TVs that picked up the ever-present BBC.

She felt sheepish. She had been clear why she had come along that afternoon, why she'd anted up for the tourist permit and driver fee that allowed them to be squired across the island. The Brit wanted the spice farm tour in the north near Mangapwani. He'd got it. She'd lobbied hard for the ocean.

The van rattled forward on a muddy potholed road through a small village. They passed women swathed in bright kangas, printed with red, black, and ochre, some with their bare feet hennaed for weddings. Others carried fruit in baskets woven from coconut palm leaves or sped by sitting side-saddle on the back of mopeds driven by nimble men wearing skullcaps. Spindly Australian pines, cut and stripped clean of bark, lay like stacks of giant toothpicks against low cement-block com-pounds, waiting to be used as building poles. I have to get back here, thought Regina. No more drive-by filmmaking.

The clouds huddled tighter in the distance, ready to pounce, and yet out by the road all was lively and indifferent.

"I'd like to live here," she'd said to the Brit. It felt harmless enough. They'd been drinking Tuskers on a patio in Zanzibar a few hours after they'd landed and unpacked. He'd showed her a wallet-photo of his young Russian wife, whose hard eyes were set in a girlishly pale face, and who waited for him in their London home. She'd let her guard drop. "But I wouldn't do it if it meant living in some gated expat community."

"You're white. So you're privileged. You'd want things too, like air conditioning. You wouldn't be safe. You couldn't live outside of a gate."

"It would be neat," she said, "to try."

It was a throw away comment, ill-considered.

His eyes lit up, a kind of ugly glee in them.

"Neeeet," he said so that his lips stretched into a mocking grin. "You thought it would be neeet."

From the taxi window, Regina watched the almond and mango trees part for an expanse of coral rag. The road beyond it was bumpier still. The sky, still dark, moved restlessly. Everybody else was dozing. She could not sleep in moving vehicles. But the Brit was an accomplished napper. She looked at his bespectacled face and saw the little boy he had once been. A little prince with a flaccid chin. It would have been easy to pick on him, she thought stretching out her long legs under the seat ahead. I would have picked on him. Mercilessly.

She sensed water was near. Coconut palms made a row of exclamation points on the horizon and soon she could make out the modest guest houses of Jambiani. The rains had yet to break. When the van slowed down to wind through the palms, the rest of the crew – an Austrian sound man, a British editor, the Swedish science broadcaster who was slated to be narrator – awoke, surprised to have made it to the other side of the island.

They emptied out of the van groggily and took the path to the beach through a cluster of grass-thatched huts. A man sat on a bench below a palm tree beside a little boy. The van driver spoke to him. He looked at the strangers coldly, and then waved them forward.

"*Jambo*," Regina said to him while walking past.

He gave a flat "*Jambo*" in reply.

"*Habari?*" she persisted.

"*Nzuri.*"

"*Ahsante sana.*"

Her cheerleader enthusiasm for guidebook Swahili phrases chafed the Brit too. She could tell. On the farms near the Jozani forest, the children had giggled with delight, and the shy women holding babies on their hips smiled when she greeted them with her few words. But now the man looked at her warily. The Brit snorted. She shrugged it off. Beyond her were a lip of white sand and the azure water of the Indian Ocean. The trip wouldn't be a total bust.

On the beach were a few lounge chairs and some skinny dogs snoozing in the cool sand beneath them. The horizon line was dotted with wooden dhows. She had read they fished for octopus here. She resisted sharing this information with the others.

Sunlight slipped through a peephole of dark clouds. She moved quickly, dropping her jeans and T-shirt in a little trail behind her, before plunging into the water like a kid, falling helplessly into the silk of its little waves. It was shallow and warm, and its saltiness crept into her mouth like a trickle of fresh blood.

"So is there a push to get rid of your Queen?" he'd asked her earlier.

"What do you mean?" she'd said.

"Last time I checked you had a queen," he said.

"A queen?" she repeated and then realized with a giggle she'd forgotten that Canada was still a monarchy. Queen, Senate, Commons. Despite the repatriated constitution and a regent's utter irrelevance.

"We don't think much about the Queen in Canada," she retorted but it was too late. He had caught her again. And later she would hear his vinegar-soaked voice repeat how this Canuck did not even know she lived in a monarchy.

She made little dolphin-dives in and under the water until something scraped her thigh. When she peered downward she saw row after row of stakes and waving fingers of plant life. It was a seaweed farm. She'd read about this too. She began to navigate between stakes to move beyond the beds with a gentle breaststroke. In the distance, she could see breakers where the shallows ended and the dhows bobbed. She wanted to reach the deeper water. She eased into a front crawl.

The sun had slipped like a hot dime through the opening in the clouds. She looked behind her. A few of the others had straggled into the water. And there was the Brit moving toward her fast in an awkward half-swim, half-wading bob. He was shirtless, his slight shoulders like a young boy's, his belly white and soft. She stopped beyond the seaweed beds and let her feet drop to the bottom to test the depth. Her head was submerged. She waited for him, treading water, but he just pushed right past her.

"Beautiful isn't it?" she said.

"Hmm."

"I think those breakers are farther away than they look."

He didn't answer. Perhaps he didn't hear. But she wondered. She swam forward a bit, parallel to him, and flipped on to her back like an otter and looked up into the sky. More clouds were muscling in from the west.

Two weeks earlier in an Addis Ababa hotel room, hours after a meal of Nile perch washed down with fermented mango, she began to vomit. Her head pounded. In the morning, they found her too weak to get out of bed. They left her there. It was the Brit's call and he made it quickly. He ordered them to dump the heavy equipment in her hotel room, while she lay prone. For three days, she lay alone staring at BBC Africa. She moved the wastebasket from the bathroom, so she could throw up without leaving the bed. Her knees shook when she rose for a glass of water. Her head swam.

And she had time to picture the Brit and the others in white sports utility vehicles descending from the dry plains into the emerald glove of the Great Rift Valley. She dreamed they passed hornbills poking under acacias like small men in black suits with bad intentions. And they didn't know what they were looking at. She imagined they were relieved to have jettisoned the Canuck with the weak stomach and the penchant for naming species.

In Arba Minsch, they hired a Nigerian pilot with a Cessna to fly them to the capital and save them the drive back. She met them at the airport with all the equipment, shaky knees, a wan smile, and her best version of a stiff upper lip. She had no energy to waste on resentment. On the flight to Kilimanjaro that afternoon, she was throwing up in the washroom as the plane landed. During the descent, the clouds had parted for a stunning view of the summit, the Austrian told her later.

Regina made a last surge toward the breakers, passing the Brit easily, and squinting her eyes at him. She could tell he was not a good swimmer, by the way he was moving. She could tell he was not reading the signs of the water.

But what could she say to him? He was not a man who took advice from over-enthusiastic women, especially Canadian women. She watched his choppy strokes. Regina had the urge to shout out to him her c.v. with water. Dove into northern lakes with dark bottoms. Bodysurfed cold Atlantic waves. Smacked hard by bully undertows. Survived a skin-purpling plunge through ice.

She decided he wouldn't be impressed.

Regina flipped over, looked for the Brit. What is he trying to prove? she thought. She called to him.

"Wind's picking up. Watch the clouds."

He did not look back. He was working toward the breakers. The water was deeper, the waves grew. He was tiring out.

She turned herself around and looked toward the beach. The others were waving them in.

"We need to go back."

She'd yelled it angrily. He turned around. She pointed to the clouds and then the beach. She waited for him. She noticed the current pushing him on a diagonal farther away from her. She began to swim slowly toward the beach, staying parallel with the Brit. Watching him but trying not to make it too obvious. He would be irritated with her, indignant.

On the trip, the Brit had assumed the seats beside the politicians and academics. He spoke Russian to the Soviet-schooled Ethiopian researchers. He got his questions answered first and interrupted, ever so politely, when someone spoke to her, if he still needed a point clarified.

He'd showed a pleasant boredom with Africa and this more than anything made Regina seethe. He'd been before. "Five times, actually," he'd said even though neither she nor any of the others had asked. So why can't he speak a phrase of Swahili? she'd thought. Why can't he name a damn bird?

Regina peeked over again. His stroke was looking ragged. He was wasting energy keeping his head entirely out of the water. She let the current push her nearer to him. When she got within a few yards, she thought she saw panic in his face. He had stopped swimming and was flailing a bit, pushing his face into the water, and then jerking forward.

The sky had become a black bruise. The dhows were back in shore. Regina drew in a breath, lunged forward and dove under the water, opening her eyes to find his pale skin's luminescence in the murk. She grabbed his leg, the one that wasn't moving, felt down it with her hands to where the seaweed clump and rope had tangled him. She pulled up the stake and then ripped the rope from it. He kicked. The leg was free. He kicked again quickly and hit Regina in the jaw.

Regina pushed up for air. A wave rolled over them. She shut her mouth a second too late and swallowed a gulp of water.

The waves were rougher now but they were only a few yards from the shallows. Regina frog-kicked with a last, manic energy.

The Austrian and Swede had run into the waters to help. Regina's heart was pounding. She stopped swimming to find her footing on the sand underneath. She was just about to start wading when the men reached her. Each man hooked a hand under each of her underarms and pulled her to her feet.

"No," she protested. "I'm okay!"

She turned her head around. The Brit had made it to the shallows. He was wading back in, panting, and pale. He was standing on his own. He did not look at her.

The rain came in hard lashing lengths as they reached the sand. They ran for the shelter of a thatched hut that had been converted to a beach-side bar.

Inside, she wrapped herself with a towel. The Austrian producer shook himself like a mad puppy.

"You shouldn't have gone that far if you couldn't handle it," he snapped.

Regina turned to the Brit. He was laughing with the Swede, the hue of relief colouring his face. He was turned away from her.

She found her things and a dark corner where she could change. Her jaw throbbed. She felt tears but willed them to hold. I saved him, she thought. I saved the bastard.

Outside the wind bent the palms into tall walking canes. The rain beat the hut, shook the walls.

The others were sitting around a table. They had ordered beers. They started talking about how the documentary – its editing, post-production, grants – would be completed once they got home. She sat with them. They did not stop talking. The Brit's eyes never wandered near hers.

A tattooed German girl came from behind the bar and asked her if she would like a drink, and Regina nodded. She drank two beers in quick succession. I will have to start all over when I get back, she thought. In her head she made an inventory of the calls she would make, the money left in her savings account.

They ran for the taxi waiting for them in the shelter of the palms. The giddy rain pounded down as they left Jambiani. They passed men in white cotton shirts walking alongside the road who let the downpour soak through to their skin, splash their cheeks and eyes as if it was air, as if it was not tangible.

A contented snore underscored the silent humidity inside the van. Nobody spoke. Regina did not look to see who was sleeping. It rained all the way back to the Stone Town and stopped abruptly as twilight fell. There was nothing to say, not even when the air filled with mist, and there appeared a rainbow of intense vermillion and shimmering gold that made an ambitious arc over the water, the length of Zanzibar.

ANDREW J. BORKOWSKI

TWELVE VERSIONS OF LECH

X.

I still look up to Lech's second-floor window whenever I pass. During those times when he wouldn't answer the door he'd be there, perched over the street, chin in hand, staring down the gargoyles of St. Voytek's Church. On Sundays I'd look up guiltily as I slunk out of Mass behind my parents and I could see him framed in the bay window, my judge and saviour, improbably balanced on the back of a chair.

X.

A big man in neutral clothes, trousers held up with rope and hair like an overturned stork's nest. Lech extended a broad hand and asked, "Does your father smoke a pipe?"

"Why yes," I said. "He does."

And then Lech just walked away before I could shake with him.

Yola had prepared his way. She told us about Lech's canvasses and prints hanging in the Prado, at MoMA, and in the Pompidou. She told us how Magritte helped him defect after he won the 1962 biennale in Brussels. An artist was loose on Copernicus Avenue, the real thing. He was the kind of artist our parents were certain not to like, an escape artist who had given gravity the slip.

X.

"When you get down to nothing, *that's* when you got something."

The emptiness of Lech's flat could make your head spin. The smell of dust baking on iron radiators. No bedroom. No backrests on any of the chairs except the one that sat in the front window. CBC programmes murmured from a clock radio twenty-four hours a day, backed by the click of mechanical digits flipping over every sixty seconds. Sills and door jambs sagged under a weight of paint.

By the telephone, a plastic cup shaped like Jiminy Cricket, with eyes that followed you as you inspected his prints. *Objects at the Speed of Nothing*, he called them, swaths of cool colour sweeping over one another. They were expressions of "reductionism," which was an advancement, he claimed, on the "anti-velocitarian" movement he founded in Krakow in the fifties. The anti-velocitarians would paint themselves white then lie in groups of twenty across the lengths of canvas on which the art college forced them to paint portrait after identical portrait of Stalin. They staged "manifestations of immobility" to block major intersections, market squares, and the forecourts of state enterprises. They incited workers to "acts of stillness" with instruction cards printed in letters so small that the police couldn't read them. Neither, of course, could the workers.

"So," Lech concluded, eyes gleaming with mischief, "Anti-velocitarianism accomplished exactly nothing. That was a great, great success!"

X.

He was a fabulous liar and to prove it he threw himself down on a park bench next to an American couple perspiring cheerfully into identical wool suits.

After some pleasantries about the hot Canadian summer that the Americans had not expected, the husband leaned confidentially into Lech and said, "You're not from around here, are you?"

Lech raised his hands in surrender. "And how do you *know* that?"

"Oh, I can tell by your accent," the American chuckled. "You're one of those *French* Canadians aren't you?"

"Actually no. You are wrong."

"I am? Then what are you?"

"I," Lech announced, "am a Laplander."

The American nodded as if a nagging doubt had been solved at last. His wife laid a hand on Lech's knee.

"I've always wondered," she said. "Do you people pay income tax?"

"We do," Lech confessed. "We pay it in bones."

X.

"Here."

It's a black-and-white glossy snapshot, edges serrated like a postage stamp. Lech's hair is pure black and has yet to thin at the crown. His grin is softened with awe as it faces the unmistakable moustachios and mad stare of the elderly man across the café table from him: Dali.

"This was taken the day before Dali got me my refugee status in Barcelona. He spoke no Polish, I spoke no Catalan, so I looked at him across the table and said in English, 'Does your father smoke a pipe?'"

Was it Dali or Magritte? Barcelona or Brussels? And was it true that he had married his way into Canada and had a wife and daughter in Montreal? What about his family in Poland? Weren't there consequences back then for the relatives of defectors?

Rumours seeped through the footings of all his relationships. We wanted more. We wanted facts, a truth we could trust, and to be trusted, as equals, with the truth. But if you pressed Lech too hard you risked banishment.

"Journalist!" he would hiss. And you'd be banished for weeks to the sidewalk below his window.

X.

Yola Skarpinski served tea among her unsold copies of Gide and Zola while we talked, as always, about Lech.

"Has he told you," she asked, "about the day he came

home from school and found all his neighbours hanging from lamp posts?"

Nobody spoke.

"Is that true?" I asked.

Yola smiled as she screwed a Sobranie into her amber cigarette holder. "Perhaps not – but it could be. You can never know what happened to Lech. It is a silent agreement we all have with ourselves, that nothing will ever make us prisoners again, not even a memory."

X.

"Go get us some nice cake."

He said it as if we had been arguing about cake for years. I took his twenty dollar bill, went to Pani Wysotska's bakery and bought a cheesecake. Something was up. Lately he had been setting more than the usual number of loyalty tests, pranks meant to drive us away. A week earlier, while they argued about the validity of society as poetical concept, Lech had served my brother Blaise multiple shots of *spiritus* in glasses of herb tea with honey. Lech said this was "the traditional way" to drink *spiritus* in his part of Poland. The tea turned out to be a laxative.

When I brought the cheesecake back to Lech, he stared at the ten-inch slab in disbelief. Wordlessly he went to the kitchen, came back with a fork, and handed it to me along with the cake box.

"You *bought* that whole thing!" he said. "So now you gonna *eat* that whole thing!"

I stopped my throat with creamy curds until I was too heavy to lift myself.

I would have eaten fifty cakes that afternoon. Just to show him.

X.

He liked to watch the phone ring until the caller gave up, then make bad jokes about who it might have been: a trunk call from Hannibal and his elephants, Richard Nixon inviting us to a taping, Leonid Brezhnev using a Party line.

"But what if it's something important?" I asked him once.

He just looked at me as if I'd lost my mind.

The longest time I ever saw him on the phone he didn't say a word. He sat on the floor, as if to conduct the caller's voice into the shag carpet with minimum resistance through limp appendages. Then he turned the receiver into the room so that I could hear the woman's voice meandering inside it. She spoke Polish, soft runs of consonants, cadences of heartbreak that the language frames so well. Lech let me hear every word as the woman bared her soul in the tongue I had grown up surrounded by and still didn't understand.

After she had hung up he said, "Aleksei, the artist must be completely selfish."

X.

Lech kissed Therese's hand in the manner of my father's generation and said, "So Aleksei, I finally meet your attachment."

Then he thrust a folio of his *InAction* lithographs at her as if he was serving a summons. Hugging the folio, Therese retreated to the window over the street, to the chair with the back on it, where no one but Lech ever sat. Lech stayed in the kitchen the whole time, scrubbing plates that never left the sink with a two-bit-sized scouring pad. The harder he scrubbed, the longer Therese took to pour over the lithographs. She sat with legs crossed, the free foot jiggling impatiently the way it still does whenever she's forced to suffer fools. Finally she brought the folio back to the kitchen and set it in the drying rack saying, "Have you ever drawn a baby? Or an apple?"

X.

"I have devised a spectacle for you and your beautiful young lady," he said. "It is called The Spectacle of Adam and Eve. There will be a beautiful music and chanting. We will fill the room with incense. Then you and your young lady will come to the stage. You will remove each other's clothes, cover yourselves in oils, and make beautiful love. And we gonna do that in the church hall of the St. Voytck's! Now how 'bout that?"

"Sure, Lech."

I humoured him for a whole month as he regaled me with plans for the lighting, sets, and music. Then I panicked when he showed me a signed contract for the hall.

"I'm not going through with it, Lech. I – I just can't."

Lech smiled his little smile and put a hand on my shoulder. "So. Now we know," he said.

X.

Some lunatic had shot the Pope. Within hours of the shooting, the ground in front of his statue at the entrance to the Parish Trust was littered with flowers. I bought a single carnation and was furtively laying it on the pile when Lech emerged from the Trust office clutching a hydro bill in his left hand. The hand skittered behind his back, as if he was embarrassed to be caught paying a bill. But he recovered quickly enough when he realized what I was doing.

"Does this bother you, what has happened to *Il Papa*?"

"Of course," I said. "Doesn't it bother you?"

"Why should it? They always kill the popes. Haven't you heard of Luc-r-r-r-ezia Borgia? She poisoned *three* of them. Her brothers!"

"But today . . ."

"Aha! You think because today we have garbage disposal and air conditioning this will not happen. Come on. I show you something."

Lech steered me down the length of Copernicus Avenue, bobbing among shoppers moored to the boxes of fruit and cheap underwear in front of the shops. We reached the bottom of the street where it widens into a multi-veined delta of streetcar tracks. At first, I thought he was taking me to the Katyn monument, but he brushed past the cleft bronze monolith with its candles dissolving in the sun. The Sunnyside Bridge vaulted us toward the blue skies over Lake Ontario, then set us down outside the Palais Royale. Around back of the old dance hall, on the sand at the water's edge, Lech stretched out his arms and offered himself to the place where the blue of the water met the blue of the air.

"Did you know Austrian was the first language of Kanada?"

"No."

"Yes. Do you know what the Indians said – in Austrian – when your Jacques Cartier asked what was the name of this place?"

"Canada."

"Exactly. Ka-na-da. And in Austrian this means *Keine dar* – 'nobody's there.'"

"I thought it meant 'village of small huts' or 'swamp' or something."

"No, you are *wrong*. Because nobody thought about asking what those words mean until after they killed all the Indians with the smallpox. What you think about that? You live in a country where nobody knows what its name means. Do you read your great Canadian critics of literature?"

"No."

Lech swelled with pleasure at the lapse in my scholarship.

"They say the great question for you is 'Where is here?' So now you got the answer to that question. The Indians give it to you. You know where is here?"

"No, Lech. Why don't *you* tell me where is here?"

"Here," he said, "is nowhere. And that, Aleksei, is a good, good place to be."

He turned to the lake and sang out in his roisterous baritone.

"KA-NA-DA."

I followed his gaze to the vanishing point where, for the first time, I saw the inspiration for his *Objects at the Speed of*

Nothing. I saw how the void had beckoned to him in a world murderous with ideas. Lech waded into the algae-clotted shallows my mother had always warned us about, his untucked shirt billowing like a sail. As I watched his reflection scatter in the surf, I felt anchored and old. At the same time, I realized that I and all the spiritual expeditionists of Copernicus Avenue were too young for the world that Lech had known.

We probably always would be.

CRAIG BOYKO

OZY

1:	1500000	WWJ
2:	1200000	NEF
3:	1000000	RTP
4:	750000	BQD
5:	500000	TYO
6:	250000	GMV
7:	150000	DSA
8:	100000	HIV
9:	75000	THG
10:	50000	MKE

The scores were fake. They were too even, too rounded. Tenth place, bottom rung, was exactly 50,000 points. Ninth was exactly 75,000. Eighth exactly 100,000. Fifth was not a point more nor less than half a million. First place would cost you exactly one and a half million.

"It's goddamn impossible," said my brother after his first game. He'd scored 17,455.

If the highest scores seemed too big, the lowest were too small. The top ten were spaced out in neat exponential increments, like currency or prizes.

I was old enough to know that progress was made not in great, smooth leaps but in clumsy, painful steps. I'd played piano for six months, taken swimming lessons for three, and been a scout for about two weekends – and if I'd ever found myself stranded on an island twelve metres from the mainland with nothing but a Swiss Army knife and a Casiotone keyboard, I'd have died of hunger or poison ivy in about twelve hours flat and wouldn't even have been able to perform my own funeral dirge.

Genius was not a gift. Talent was not innate. Practice, and only practice, made perfect – which was just to say that the long road to perfection was paved with bumpy, potholed imperfection. If some kid calling himself "WWJ" had really scored 1,500,000 points, there should have been countless others who'd only done 1,450,000, 1,464,000, 1,485,975. For every Edmund Hillary who reached the peak, there should have been dozens of frozen carcasses littering the mountain-side below. The lack of evidence of any such carnage in the hygienic high score list was proof of its artificiality.

And that offended something in me. I was insulted. And I'd learned from my brother a useful self-defense manoeuvre: Take every insult as a challenge.

I told him to give me a goddamn quarter.

"Suck a turd, midget."

I could tell by the mildness with which he said it that he was out of money. So were the others. We lingered around the machine like smitten suitors, jiggling its joysticks and tapping its buttons, already reminiscing over past exploits and sketching out the fiery mayhem we would unleash in the near future, until Mr. Kacvac, invoking his dead wife's long-suffering soul, told us to get out of the store. Our loitering was scaring away paying customers.

Everyone but me had great handles. Some – Donnie Werscezsky (DON), James Lorenson (JIM), and my brother (LEO), to name but a few – had been blessed from birth with names exactly three letters long. Others – Gob McCaffrey and Pud Milligan, for instance – had had such names bestowed upon them by inadvertently generous peers. Even those whose names seemed at first glance to be as unabbreviatable as my own had little difficulty re-christening themselves. Hank Lowenthal, who occasionally claimed British heritage and could quote entire scenes from *Monty Python and the Holy Grail* as proof, embraced his pedigree with ANK. Sanjeet Kastanzi, who everyone called Sanj, had a number of options: SAN was safe if rather dull, ANJ was bold if a little risky, and KAS had a nice rough-and-tumble ring to it. (SNJ was tacitly off-limits; we all wanted our names to be sayable.) In the end he went – a little overweeningly, I thought – with JET.

And Theodore Mandel, a friend of my brother's, tried on labels like they were shoes. Indeed, I sometimes suspected that the challenge of textual condensation was the only reason he played – just as I sometimes suspected that the only reason he hung around with Leo was so he could refer to the pair of them in rhyming third person.

Theo tried on TEO first, then DOR. But you could see the dissatisfaction of the artist in his eyes. When he discovered that numerals were permissible, he came up with 3OH ("Three-oh"), 3A4 ("Three-a-four"), and finally, his *chef d'oeuvre*, OEO. The zero, he explained to everyone in the grocery store, stood for the Greek letter theta which, in the International Phonetic Alphabet, was the symbol for the "th" sound. We responded to this little lesson with a different sound. Marcel Kacvac (MUT), who we all looked up to in fear and awe because he had a tattoo, a car, and acne, started calling Theo "Oreo," and then, because "Oreo" was not offensive enough to ever catch on, "Cookie." But Theo defused the danger by pretending to be delighted. For a week, he insisted that everyone call him Cookie and for a week, everyone refused. "Piss off, *Theo*" even became a schoolyard catchphrase. I used it to greet him one night at the door to our walk-up and was swatted for it later by my mom, who, seated upstairs in the kitchen, had neither heard him call me "Oozy" first, nor seen him playfully ruffle my hair afterwards.

I was supposed to have been OLD. O.L.D. really were my initials. Fortuitously, they spelled a recognizable word. And old was something I wanted to be anyway. OLD was perfect.

I crept onto the high-score screen with my very first quarter. Naturally, I took this to be an omen, a sign that I'd been earmarked for greatness. But my triumph was short-lived.

LEO – whose hard-won 76,450 points had been propelled into the abyss by my seemingly effortless 78,495 – immediately pantsed me. This was to be expected, and wouldn't even have been humiliating if Mrs. Schrever, my brother's History teacher, hadn't been in the store at the time. Because she was, Mr. Kacvac felt obliged to loudly reprimand my brother and me for our deplorable behaviour. Normally, he didn't give a damn how we comported ourselves so long as merchandise got paid for. He believed Mutt's generation to be so far beyond redemption that it didn't even trouble him anymore. On the contrary, he seemed to relish each fresh confirmation of our wickedness. When there were no adult customers in the store, he encouraged us to deride volunteerism, team sports, and homework. Once, home from school with a feigned illness, I wandered into his store in the middle of a weekday afternoon and Kacvac rewarded my waywardness with a free handful of gummie fruits. But that day, with Mrs. Schrever in the store, he had to condemn my brother's wanton cruelty and my obscene immodesty until the grown-up finally paid and left.

The charge of willful obscenity was, I thought, a little unfair. It's not that I wouldn't, but *couldn't* pull up my pants right away. There was a high score that needed claiming; I had to enter my initials first.

Whether in my excitement or because everyone was laughing at the threadbare state of my skivvies, I overshot the D and put an E in its place. The mistake proved irrevocable. So I pretended I hadn't made a mistake at all. When Saul Lasburgh demanded to know what the heck "Olé" was supposed to mean, I just shrugged enigmatically but with tight-lipped significance, as though we were really talking about some girl I'd banged, and whom I was too much of a gentleman, or depraved pervert, to slander by disclosing the garish details.

In the end, it didn't matter. My low high score was wiped out, to my secret relief, a mere twenty minutes later by DON. OLE was dust.

But so was OLD. That name was now forever tainted. It was just as well, I realized. OLD was a stupid, terrible name. Mrs. Schrever was old. Mr. Kacvac was old. And did I really want it getting out that my middle name was Leslie?

OSS seemed the obvious choice but I didn't like it. It looked amputated. Standing on their own like that, the first three letters of my name gave no clue to their origin, their context, their pronunciation. Future generations would suppose that OSS rhymed with *floss* or *gloss* – words not known to strike fear into the human heart.

I could fix this problem by substituting Zs for the double-S but I didn't like OZZ any better. It looked ugly and asymmetrical, the second Z was technically superfluous. Besides, I hated "Oz," with all its childish connotations: witches, wizards, and flying monkeys, munchkins and a yellow brick road, a girl named Dorothy and a dog named Toto, for crying out loud. Yes, I had made a habit of kicking the shins of anyone who called me Oz and who was not my brother.

So what did that leave?

OSI? OZI? OZE?

Ossie's needs had been modest. He'd spent his meagre allowance on little more than junk food, model airplanes, elastic bands, and paper clips – which he and Philip O'Toole (POT) stopped firing at human targets after Jill Alistair's mom complained to their moms.

OZY, on the other hand, was always on the lookout for money.

I dismantled our sofas. I stuck my fingers inside payphones and pop machines. I trawled the gutters in our neighbourhood with my eyes. At night, I stole quarters from my mother's purse and, in the morning, obfuscated my crime by demanding an advance on my allowance. (After all, no thief in his right mind would return to his victim the very next day as a supplicant.) I upturned my peanut butter jar and converted its contents, my life savings, into a roll of pennies, two rolls of nickels, and a roll of dimes – nine dollars and fifty cents in all. At the bank, I watched, red-faced, as the teller removed, with a long red fingernail, two quarters from a roll before cheerfully handing it over to me. It felt like a slap on the hand. But my mood improved as soon as I stepped back out on the street with thirty-eight quarters in my pocket, weighing the left side of my cords down almost past my hip.

Unfortunately, there was no one in Kacvac's but Kacvac. I felt the need to flourish my fortune at someone, so I squandered one play – three whole lives – on a dozen gummie fruits. Fussily, but with good-humoured resignation, like someone who has grown weary of the bank's empty promises to make their coins easier to get at, I peeled a coin from the top of my roll and slid it across the counter like a checkers pro.

"Mazel Tov," said Mr. Kacvac gloomily, and in his perpetually damp eyes I saw not the dysfunction of lachrymal glands (a medical condition that my mother had warned me not to mention) but a keen, unadulterated – and unadult – envy.

In no hurry to shatter my adversaries' records in their absence, I sauntered up to the machine, performed a few limbering calisthenics, looked around the store, smiled companionably back at Mr. Kacvac, peeled off another quarter, and inserted it into the slot. The machine chimed happily, like a baby robot gurgling at the sight of its mother. I exchanged a grim nod with my reflection in the store window, like two rugged highwaymen crossing paths out on some lonely mesa after midnight. Then I reached up over my head, gripped the joystick with one hand, and slapped the START button with the other.

It was not respect that we sought. Those who were better than you could not respect you, and those who were worse could not even like you. Those who did not play – my mother, our teachers, the President of the United States of America – did not really exist.

It was not respect that we were after but immortality. I dreamed of taking all ten high scores. I dreamed of an army of OZYS slaughtering anyone who would deny them their rightful place in eternity.

It never occurred to us that our high scores might not be immortal. They were as indelible as a Guinness World Record or the Permanent File that Principal Ballsack kept locked in the cabinet in his office – and which he promised to show no one but such colleges, potential employers, and juries as might someday need to be disabused of any notion of our goodness or worth. Our high scores were the high scores of all time and space. We assumed they would last forever.

For disabusing us of this notion, Roger Pembroke (ROG) was systematically ostracized. We put dead gophers in his locker, we squashed his lunches with our textbooks, we tied his gym shoes together and wrapped them around the football goalpost like a bola, and then – worst of all – we left him alone.

ROG had been one of the real contenders, one of the Obliterati. He'd been with us from the beginning. He'd been the first to "get HIV," with 104,895 points. He'd also been the first to kill the underwater level boss – a giant robotic octopus that sprayed clouds of ink that would freeze you to your spot for five seconds while it – rather implausibly, I thought – lobbed fireballs at you.

Leo smacked me in the side of the head and said that obviously *grease* fires could burn underwater. Phil, who was supposed to be my best friend, backed him up, saying that everybody knew that the army had flame-throwers on their attack subs. I asked if he meant the navy, and Leo smacked me again.

"*Ow* – what was that for?"

"For being a smartass."

"I wasn't," I said truthfully. (*Wasn't* it the navy who had subs?) I felt the first prickle of tears gathering somewhere beneath the skin of my cheeks. It was not hardship or cruelty but injustice that made me emotional.

"Oh shit. I was just teasing. Don't pull a Kacvac on us."

One afternoon, Roger was in striking distance of usurping Jack Thomas (TOM) for sixth place. We were all cheering him on. Jack Thomas was almost eighteen and, like MUT, far too old, in our opinion, to be competing. Shouldn't he have girls to bang? we asked ourselves.

This was approximately one month after the machine had first appeared in Kacvac's, dumped indifferently, as though by some giant stork, at the front of the store between the rotating display of birthday cards and the three shopping carts that no one ever used because they were too wide for all but the frozen foods aisle. None of us ever really paused to wonder where the game had come from. Though battered and scuffed with age and rough use, it seemed to us to have simply materialized out of thin air, like some sort of divine challenge – like Arthur's sword in the stone. Some of us must have realized that Mr. Kacvac owned Kacvac's, but he never seemed like anything but a worn-out and mistreated employee in his own store. It was inconceivable that we had him to thank for *Ballistic Obliteration*.

A month after it appeared, the bottom five scores were history. MKE was long forgotten. THG's thing had fallen off. DSA had, of course, caught AIDS from HIV. We were unable to do much with GMV or TYO – which was suspicious. Indeed, with the exception of HIV, none of the default high scorers' names spelled anything even remotely dirty. They even seemed to have been chosen to rule out offensive acronyms. Not a single DIK or TIT or AZZ among them – another sure sign that they were fakes.

Then again, none of us ever resorted to such vulgarity either. We took the game, and our fame, too seriously. To pass up the chance to take personal credit for your score would be more than a tragic waste; it would be a gesture of disrespect, more obscene than any three-letter word could be. Lennie Gruman (LEN) – who later became my principal rival, next to Fran Tate (FT) – did once enter POO after losing three lives in quick succession to the dragon on the lava level (who at least did not breathe water at you). But no one so much as smiled at POO. It had been a gesture of peevishness, we all knew, not rebelliousness. LEN had two better scores on the list already, so maybe it didn't matter. But there were kids – my brother, for one – who'd have killed for what Lennie tossed so dismissively aside – namely, 589,140 points.

At the time of ROG's last game, the bottom five scores were 545,770, 532,225, 528,445, 500,000, and 476,610. They belonged to TOM, FT, OZY, the imaginary TYO, and ROG himself. Watching him play were FT, OZY, POT, and Wally Hersch, who never had a moniker because he never made it onto the high scores list. The kid was hopeless. His hand and his eye were apparently operated by different brains altogether. And he never got any better despite all the quarters he plugged into the machine. We serious players respected neither his ineptitude nor his conspicuous wealth, so we never let him play unless we were all broke or he promised to lend us money, which he did gladly for anyone who would play doubles with him. But this we refused to do.

Two-person play was, at least among the Obliterati, tacitly prohibited. It was easier to get further when playing doubles, and while the points that piled up had to be split two ways, the extent of player one's contribution to player two's success and vice versa could never be teased apart. Doubles scores were an inaccurate and therefore invalid measure of one's skill. A high score that came out of a doubles game was deemed not just worthless but in fact immoral, because every illegitimate score displaced a legitimate one. It didn't matter if your partner *was*

Wally – that is, if he contributed nothing, if he died off before you even got as far as the wild boar boss at the end of the forest level. It was a question of precision. Of honour.

I once walked into Kacvac's to find Lennie Gruman playing alone. I watched him mutely for ten minutes. Suddenly, he let out a shriek and swiftly committed hari kari.

"Why the hell'd you do that?" I wanted to know. "You were creeping up on bottom rung with two damn lives left."

"No shit. Why d'you think I killed myself?"

Evidently Mutt Kacvac had been labouring over the machine when Lennie came into the store. MUT never played if anyone was around. He didn't like being watched. He was not a real contender, and he concealed his lack of skill behind a mask of derisive indifference. When Lennie came in, he suddenly remembered he had to be somewhere and asked LEN if he wanted to take over. Lennie hesitated, so Mutt casually crashed his ship into a toxic chemical vortex, then turned and strode out of the store without another word. Lennie couldn't bear to let most of a quarter go to waste. But nor could he claim a high score that was not completely, one hundred percent his own. When he backed away from the machine after his *felo de se*, he kept shaking his hands as though they were dripping wet and muttering to himself, "That was close, that was a real close call."

By the time Jack Thomas came into the store, Roger had 521,915 points. He'd secured ninth place and was sneaking up on me in eighth. He'd made it to the electricity level – a nightmare landscape of sparkling capacitators and fizzling dynamos swept with gleaming acid showers and arc lightning that only a few of us had ever seen with our own two eyes – and he'd done it without losing a single life. He had 521,915 points, his Faradization upgrade, ten nukes, a triple forcefield, and three ships left. He was on fire.

Fran, Phil, Wally and I fell silent. Even the buzzing coolers in the produce section seemed to hold their breath. TOM, our current scoring leader, pretended not to notice what was happening. He made a lazy circuit of the store like an old lady searching for discounts. He stood in front of Mr. Kacvac and deliberated out loud over which brand of cigarettes he should try today. In the end, he bought nothing but a newspaper, which he folded neatly and tucked under his arm before finally strolling, lackadaisically and as though quite by chance, in our direction.

"What's this?" he asked primly.

"It's a video game," Fran said quietly. "Never seen one?"

Casually, and with the inattentive air of someone lighting a pipe, Jack asked, "And how's old Rog doing?"

"Fine," Phil said.

"Pretty good, actually," Wally said. "He's got ninth place."

Roger muttered something under his breath.

Jack stooped forward slightly, turned his head to one side, and blinked rapidly out the window. "Hmm? What's that he said?"

"Eighth place," Fran said. "He just got eighth."

"There goes Ossie," said Wally.

I exhaled. Something tight in my chest loosened up.

"Nice one," I said.

"Holy, what kind of power-up is *that*?" asked Wally breathlessly.

"He's right on your ass, Jack," said Phil gloatingly, "and he's got three lives."

At precisely that moment, Roger's ship exploded. He swore loudly. Mr. Kacvac, perched on his stool behind the counter, looked up from his crossword puzzle and cleared his throat threateningly. (Mrs. Howard, a friend of my mother's, was palpating lettuce heads in the produce section.) Out of respect for the dead, and not because we were cowed by Kacvac, we fell silent for a minute. Jack, who'd been about to say something, let his mouth hang open, like someone anticipating a delicacy. He brought his lips together at last:

"Two," he said. You could tell the word tasted good. "Two lives left."

Phil sent Fran a quick commiserative glance. "He's on you. He's right on you. Oh man, he's – that's it. You're toast."

"Nice one," said Fran.

"He's got seventh place now," Wally explained. "He just passed Fran."

"Seventh place," said Phil, "and he's got two lives left."

Roger's ship erupted into flames. He swore. This time Kacvac cleared his throat inquisitively, as though politely inquiring which of us would most like to be kicked out first.

"You guys are goddamn jinxing me," Roger said under his breath. "Stop saying how many lives I have goddamn left."

"Why?" said Jack brightly. "What's the matter? Are we *jinxing* you?"

He was chuckling but there was an uneasiness in his voice. His eyes, like the rest of ours, were locked on the screen, where Roger's score continued to rise, bit by excruciating bit.

"How many lives do you have left anyway? One? Just one?"

As though on cue, Roger's ship hurtled into a giant electrified razor-wire barrier and blew into pieces.

He did not swear. He slammed his palms down on the buttons and spun around to glower at Jack.

Jack grinned. Fran, Phil, Wally and I gasped in horror. Roger's game wasn't over yet. He needed less than four thousand points to beat Jack and *he had turned his back on the game.*

He was back at the controls before we could scream at him, but the one- or two-second interruption proved fatal. Before he knew what was happening, his right wing had been grazed by a deadly blue will-o-the-wisp, sending a geyser of black smoke up into the poisonous atmosphere. Roger pulled away too late and too hard, overcompensating in space for what he'd failed to do in time. He rocketed from one side of the screen to the other and came too close to a giant electromagnet, a device which looked as harmless as a giant bedspring but was as deadly as a coiled cobra. The magnet pulled him in slowly, almost gently. Then it injected him with a billion volts. The screen went white.

GAME OVER

545,385 points. Seventh place.

Roger spun around. Jack was bent double, clutching his newspaper to his chest. It looked to me like he was only pretending to laugh. "You goddamn jinxed me."

Jack straightened, took a deep breath, and fanned himself with his paper. At length, he brought his eyes to focus uncertainly, as though without recognition, on Roger.

"Twice," said Roger through his teeth.

"Hey Roger," said Wally. "Your name . . ."

The game gave you thirty seconds to enter your initials. Roger had twenty left.

He made no move. Jack stopped smiling. This was serious.

Roger was going to throw his score away. He *was* throwing it away. We were watching him do it. He was hurtling toward the edge of a cliff and defying anyone to intervene. He just stood there, glaring at Jack. Jack glared back. He was angry now too.

But he was nervous as well. His eyes kept darting to the screen. Fifteen seconds.

I couldn't breathe. Wally looked ready to pee himself. Phil had to put an arm out to prevent him from rushing forward to enter the R, O, and G on Roger's behalf.

Ten seconds.

Jack flinched first. The spell was broken. A goofy, panic-stricken grin spread across his face. He lunged past Roger, dropping his newspaper, grabbed the joystick and began jiggling it madly. He managed to tap out the last letter – an M – with less than a second to spare. Then he stepped back to admire, and invite the rest of us to admire, his work.

Phil, Fran, and I were too upset to speak. Wally appeared to be working himself up to a Kacvac. Roger just peered wordlessly at the screen.

Jack sensed he'd committed a faux pas. He became defensive. "Hey, it's just a joke. He was going to waste it. Jeez, it's just a *game*."

Mr. Kacvac had time to say "Hey, you kids –" before Roger reached around behind the machine and pulled the plug out of the wall. Wally shrieked. Fran closed his eyes. Jack Thomas's face went white. Then he stepped forward and punched Roger neatly and expertly in the stomach, like a paramedic administering the Heimlich manoeuvre. Roger reeled back, then tipped forward, using his momentum to head-butt Jack in the chest. They collapsed together into the display of birthday cards. Mr. Kacvac sprang over the counter and, perhaps by invoking his dead wife's name, or perhaps by brandishing a baseball bat, convinced all of us to come back another time.

I couldn't stay away long. The next day, under the pretense of having been delegated by my mother to purchase some goat's milk, I was able on my way out – empty-handed as planned – to confirm my fears.

MKE, THG, HIV, and DSA had made miraculous recoveries.

ROG, TOM, FT, and OZY were no more.

Gone. Just like that. Without a trace. In the blink of an eye. Forever.

So what was the point?

I must have stumbled out of the store. I found myself wandering aimlessly down a street only my feet recognized.

That night, I lay in bed, struggling to fill my mind with the idea of forever. I took a single summer day spent rambling through our neighbourhood with Phil, taking apart bugs, collecting pop cans, melting popsicles on our tongues, browsing through his dad's old CB radio catalogues, practising our ventriloquism, throwing rocks at stray cats, chalking our names on sidewalks exposed to the naked sky – I took one day like that and tried to hold it in my head all at once. Then I shrunk it down to a dot, a mere speck, and populated the vacated space with a hundred dots, a thousand specks. A sandstorm of days – as many as I'd ever see in all my life. I compressed the dust cloud too, squeezed it down into a tiny cube and pushed it to the very edge of my imagination. I began lining cubes up next to it, slowly at first, only one or two at a time, to give me a chance to grasp the enormity of the addition. Then I began adding half a dozen blocks at once, then half a dozen half-dozens, then a long undifferentiated row of blocks spanning the entire width of the space behind my eyes, then half a dozen rows, then half a dozen half-dozens.

I sensed that I was cheating; for each time I moved to a higher level, the detail of the lower levels went out of focus, so that I was no longer really multiplying the multiplied multiples of multiplied multiples but just pushing around individual blocks again, solid pieces that could only regain their plurality at the cost of their unity, parts of a whole that I could not simultaneously see as wholes of yet smaller parts. But I continued until I realized that everything I'd imagined so far, every multiplication I'd performed, could itself be condensed to a single infinitesimal cube and put through the very same process, from start to finish. And *that* entire process could be taken as a unit and run through itself, and so on, and so on, forever and ever. There it was: no matter how long you imagined forever to be, your idea of it was to the real forever as a split second was to your idea of it. This truism remained true even if you took it into account when formulating your idea of forever. Even if you took *that* into account. And that. And so on, forever and ever.

Forever, then. Forever was how long dead people stayed dead. It was how long my dad and my mom's dad and my aunt Sherona and Leo's hamster, Delorna, and Theo Mandel's mother and Jill Alistair's brother Geoff and Mr. Kacvac's wife, Eleanora, would stay dead. Forever was how long gone things stayed gone. It was how long my switchblade would stay at the bottom of Konomoke Lake, how long my magnifying glass would stay smashed (thanks, Leo), how long the key I'd lost to our old apartment building would stay lost, how long our cool old car would stay sold to a fat salesman from Wisconsin. It was how long the Alistairs' house would stay burned down, it was how long World War II would stay finished, and it was how long TOM and ROG and OZY would stay gone from the *Ballistic Obliteration* high scores list. It wouldn't matter when the power went out or when the plug was pulled. It didn't matter if it happened tomorrow or a hundred years from tomorrow. Forever would wait.

Every message is a message to the future. The feverish, grandiloquent *billet doux* stashed with trembling hand in the coat pocket of the girl you're in love with; the casual note to your wife jotted in haste and posted to the fridge before you leave in the morning; the drunken, desultory jeremiad left on your ex's answering machine – they will be read or listened to, if they are read or listened to at all, by people of the future. Even the thought scribbled carelessly in the margin of whatever novel you're reading is a variety of time travel. Every mark we make, every trace we leave is a broadcast sent out into forever. We think of our footsteps as receding behind us, but really they are beacons sent out before us.

So listen:

I was good at something once. Great, even. It was a long time ago. I was ten. Now I'm forty-three and not good at much of anything.

I'm not complaining. You're only forty-three and not good at anything for a short time. But you will have once been ten and good at something forever.

I can't prove it, of course. I have no evidence, no documentation. A month after I obliterated Fran Tate's top score by a margin that should have established my supremacy for – well, for a very long time, our neighbourhood experienced a brief power failure at about 4:30 in the morning. My mother's alarm did not go off; the three of us slept late – a real treat for Leo and me but a catastrophe for Mom, who crashed into our room bellowing and clutching her head as if bombs were being dropped on the neighbourhood.

We had to pass Kacvac's on our unhurried way to school. Power failure. Blackout. 12:00, 12:00, 12:00.

I had to go inside. Leo swore at me and continued on to school, not because he minded being late but because the decision to be late, or to do anything else, always had to be made by him.

They were gone, of course. All of them, gone forever.

Or were they? Who knows. Might there not persist, etched

upon the air we breathe, though we haven't the sensitivity to detect it or the wit to decode it, the mark of some mark, the trace of some trace?

The universe is thought to be without memory, existing only for an eternally renewed split second. Like a sprung trap, the immediate past is supposed to inexorably propel the present into the immediate future. But I think what the past really does is stand nearby, at the present's elbow, and whisper in its ear, give it counsel, suggest how a future might be made. We listen but we don't always hear everything. Not the first time. Not right away. But there might be echoes.

I put a quarter on the counter. Mr. Kacvac held out the pail of gummie fruits. I counted five, showed him. He glanced at his wristwatch. It must have been well past nine. "Oh, go on," he said. "Take a handful." And he slid my quarter back across the counter.

I stood before the machine, the coin resting in my loosely cupped palm.

Forever would wait. So, let it wait.

I dropped the quarter into my left front pocket. "Later," I promised, and hurried to school.

TOM and ROG, LEO and OEO, FT and OZY – they're gone now. Only briefly did they stir from the dust. For a short time, a time that seemed long while it lasted, they made marks that were read and left traces that were followed by others who made marks and left traces of their own. Among the marks they left were the following:

BALLISTIC OBLITERATION
** HALL OF FAME **
TOP TEN HIGH SCORES

10:	98505	MUT
9:	212005	DON
8:	299385	0EO
7:	398510	LEO
6:	545385	ROG
5:	545770	TOM
4:	784605	POT
3:	1246325	LEN
2:	1597425	FT
1:	2069100	OZY

HOW EUNICE GOT HER BABY

Eunice didn't get her baby in the usual way, through sexual intercourse with a boy in a bed, in a car, or out on the meadow after dark. Instead, she inherited her baby from the estate of her older sister Florence, through a tragedy. From the estate? Well, it wasn't really an estate, because of course there was no will made up, but when the baby became available, through the sudden accident that claimed the life of Florence, it was Eunice who was first in line. And that was a proper thing as it turned out, because Eunice was the best mother a baby could have. Better than the natural mother, some said, because Florence had a wild way about her that Eunice didn't have. Flo was impulsive and did things on a dare. Flo drove down the Trans-Canada Highway on the blackest night of the year with all the car lights turned off so she could see the stars better. Flo shut her eyes, or pretended to shut her eyes, and she crossed the busiest streets like that, with her arms stretched out. Look at me, she said, I'm a zombie. She also drank way too many beers too early on at dances, then right away she'd dance too close, and stay out way too late, past the wee hours. She'd skip classes at school the next day too, including the ones on precautions, and how she got her baby was therefore no mystery to any of her friends. Why, more often than not, Flo came home with her underpants scrunched up in her purse. That was Flo, but that was not Eunice, and that's how her little baby, Pasquena, who we all called Queenie, got lucky, sort of, when tragedy struck her mother down.

Now let's not go on too much about the wild side of Flo. There was lots that was good about her. She's got energy to burn, that's what her father said whenever he was asked. She's got her thermostat cranked up high. Her father talked like that because he had one of the best jobs on the whole Southern Shore, and that involved fuel oil. He had a yellow truck everybody recognized, and he knew everything there was to know about thermostats, and energy, and the foolish waste of heat. Some families burned their oil up twice as fast as others, he'd seen that over and over. And Flo? Well, Flo, she's like a comet, he said, there's no stopping Flo. She's fire in the sky. She burns oil. She was the oldest of all the seven children, the first in line, the experimental one, and Eunice was the baby, the last of the whole family. That meant, praise the Lord, that Eunice got insulated from the wild side of Flo by nine whole years, and all she knew about Flo was the love and the care she got from the only sister she had. Eunice always got a kiss, nothing less, no matter how late Flo got home, no matter how scrunched up Flo's underpants might have been, pushed into the top of her purse just a half-hour before. Eunice got the kisses, but she never dreamed she'd get a baby from Flo.

If she'd ever dreamed that, it would have been a nightmare. There's not too many good ways you can inherit a baby.

Even with Flo being the way she was, everything would have been fine if it hadn't been for the boy she met. His name was Darryl Bugden, and though he had lots of charms and attributes attractive to a girl, he also had the heart and the spirit of a criminal born. Not just one who picked it up along the way, for a lark with friends, but one born right to it from the word go.

How'd it happen? Flo was at the Minimart, the one she worked at on Long's Hill, reading a magazine and sitting by the cash, when she was introduced to Darryl. There was no one else in the store. It was 8 p.m., three hours to go before she closed up against the scattered few customers who came in. It was mostly cigarettes and chips and the furtive magazines for total losers, that's all.

"This here's a stick-up," was what Darryl said, his first words to her.

Flo looked up and there he was, six foot four at least, with dark curly hair and a smile despite what he said to her. All those teeth were perfect. What's with that, she thought, perfect teeth? That's rare. He did not look threatening to Flo, but how could she know, that death would appear to her in this outfit, those teeth, those words she'd only heard on TV? It never occurred to her, and it never would have occurred to anyone, looking at that smile. Anyway, it sure didn't happen right away, it took three years.

"A stick-up?" she said.

When she got the job, the boss said to her, if someone comes in and says, This is a stick-up, then you just collapse to the floor in a dead faint. Piss your pants too, that's the best.

Make as big a mess as you can and breathe like you're a spastic on the verge of a fit. Oftentimes they'll just say, Jesus Christ! and run out of the store and go somewhere else. Somehow the boss had figured that out on his own, from what happened to him once. He didn't plan it, it just happened to him and it worked. He sure didn't get that advice out of the manual that came to all the new employees, from the Downtown Merchants. In that manual, it said, just hand over all the money wordless, and do not put up any resistance. Most of these robbers are on drugs and they're twitchy, unpredictable.

It was the nice smile he had that kept her sitting there. There was no way she was going to fall to the floor and do the rest of that whole crazy drill. How bad could a girl look, no matter when?

"There's no money here. Everything bigger than a five goes right down that slot," she said.

She pointed to the wall behind her.

"Straight down into the safe."

Actually it was a slot in the wall that went straight into a cardboard liquor box that was on top of the safe. She could see it in her mind's eye, sitting there full of loose money spilling over the sides. The boss long ago forgot the number to the safe so this was a money bypass. It's a trick, he said, that fools most of them all the time.

"The safe, the combination is unknown to me," she said.

He smiled some more but he just stood there.

"The walls are three feet thick, and solid iron."

The next thing Darryl did was get over the counter. He suddenly turned and slid his butt over the plexiglass that lay over top of the lottery tickets, and there he was, he twisted around and his feet landed on the floor right beside Flo. They stood there like a couple. She got scared then, and looked out the door. Maybe there'd be a customer to come in and save her, but that was not likely. Maybe the old man with the cane or the fat lady for bubble gum, but what chance of that? There was no one in sight. And what chance would they have, anyway? None, she figured.

"Lay down on the floor," he said. Those were the next words he had with the love of his life.

Down went Flo onto the linoleum. The tiles were lifted here and there, swept just once a week so they didn't raise the dust, and she knew her white blouse, the one she bought with her own money, the one she never should have worn that night, would be ruined. Thank God for the old jeans she had on. Maybe she'd be dead soon enough anyway. It wouldn't matter then what she had on, unless there was a picture in the paper. They didn't usually show dead bodies. Even then, so what? Flo didn't care about that really. Then she lost her nerve all at once.

"There there, don't cry," said Darryl, "just shut up."

Then Darryl took his left foot and laid it down on Flo's chest near her throat while she lay there in the dirt. It was a boot like a cowboy might have, with a heel like iron maybe two inches long.

"I'm now the man at the cash tonight," he said.

He pressed his foot on her throat some, but she could still breathe.

"Don't you say a word or move," he said, "or I'll stomp on your windpipe with the toe of this boot. They got steel toes."

There was a tinkle from the door bell and she heard the shuffle-shuffle of the old man with the cane. Eight-fifteen on the button every night, for the newspaper and the dog food. Once the boss saw that the old man always got dog food, he'd marked up the cans to $2.00 for each and every one. The old guy will never notice that, he said, the old goat, the old geezer, the old fool. Later, Flo changed it back to $1.25 with the rotating stamp. The boss'll never notice that, she said, the old miser. That was the general atmosphere at the Minimart, so Darryl there behind the counter, his foot on Flo's throat, didn't really change things all that much.

"Where's Flo?" said the old man when he came up to pay.

"Underfoot somewhere, maybe in the back," said Darryl bold as brass, "I'm on the cash tonight. For all I know, she's lying down somewhere."

That's how the rest of the night was with Darryl. Flo lay on the floor but she couldn't cry anymore. Darryl took in all the cash and put none of it down the slot. After an hour went by, Darryl took off his boots with the steel toes, and just pressed on her neck with his stocking foot. She was surprised, the sock smelled clean, like wool. Whenever she looked up, he still had on that smile which never changed. He thought he was a smart-ass, she could tell, but that was common enough in all the men she knew. By nine-thirty, she no longer trembled but Darryl was none too happy with the lousy take of, so far, $38.50.

"This is one slow store," Darryl said. That foot of his seemed to move further down from her throat, down her chest until it was right on the top of her left breast. She shifted down a bit.

"Not a lot of money comes in to this dumb store," he said.

"Watch that foot please," said Flo.

"Sorry," said Darryl. He released a bit of pressure but he didn't shift the toes at all. "Is that better?"

"That's better," said Flo, but in the quiet times, between the customers, Flo thought she could feel that foot getting rhythmic on her chest. Oh well, just lay there, she figured, let it go.

"I might just close up early," said Darryl at 10:30.

"Leave now," said Flo, "there's an idea."

"Then what do I do with you?" said Darryl.

"Me?" said Flo.

"You're the eye witness," he said.

"The eye witness to what?" she said, and she thought, Oh no, this could come to a nasty turn now. Her heart began to thump so hard, under that foot on her blouse, that she thought, for sure, this guy could feel it there, thumping under his wandering toes, there was no doubt where that foot was now.

"You're the only eye witness to this crime," Darryl said. He smiled down at Flo. "I wonder, what should I do with you?"

"All those people saw you too, that came and went," she said.

"There was none of them that I saw with any kind of brain to remember," he said.

Then Flo found the way out that saved her, but in the long run, like I said before, how was she to know?

"Ask me what I saw tonight," she said. She looked up at Darryl from the floor and willed that heart of hers to stop that dreadful pounding noise it made.

"Okay, what?"

"I saw this guy, maybe five foot seven, a thin guy with rotten teeth and a weasel-face who came in and robbed the store and held me down on the floor with a gun, the whole time, and took all the money that came in until you came in at ten to eleven and chased him off."

"I did that?"

"You were brave."

"I was brave like a lion."

"Yes, you were."

"Then what happened?"

"He ran away down the hill."

"Like a rabbit."

"You mind moving that foot please to the other side?"

"Like that?"

"That's better. That's a lot better."

"How's that feel."

"That feels good." The bad part was, she wasn't lying when she said that. "You saved my life. You paid for smokes, you looked over the counter, you're tall, you saw me on the floor and you said to the guy, What's with the girl on the floor? And it was then that he pulled out his gun, forced you up against the rack of chips, and then he slipped out the door and ran and ran. You stayed with me. We made the call."

As she lay there, Florence could see the little man with the bad teeth running and running down Long's Hill, the lights from the passing cars, the sound of his footsteps getting smaller and smaller.

"What's your name?" the robber said.

"Florence."

"Florence, you get up now."

He reached down and gave her a hand up and dusted her off. He spent a lot of time on the blouse and on the upper parts of the jeans, where they were the dustiest.

Then, together, they put in the call to the Constabulary, and together they told the same story they'd worked on like they were old friends. Then they went out to George Street and drank up the money that Darryl had made that night. One thing led to another. They were both reckless to a fault. One day, it was too late for Florence, she'd missed three periods, maybe four, and little Queenie was on the way, unstoppable. The doctor said to her, I'm sorry Florence, there's no way, you're too far along for anything but to carry on with this little baby. That was okay with Flo. By then, she loved Darryl in her way, despite that smile he always had. We all warned her. Look at that guy, that smile of his. That, I think, was the worst thing we said. He could be happy, sad, busy or bored, or mean, nasty as anything, and it was always the same smile, handsome, winsome maybe to a fool, but that sick smile was forever as empty as that stupid criminal heart was of anything like kindness. Look out Florence, we said, but she never listened. She never saw it that way. It must have been how he put the sock on her chest, the knowledge he had from being older, like Flo was some kind of hostage all her life one way or another, underfoot, in the way.

You could see the writing on the wall, the late-night driving they did up and down the Number 10 Highway, the open beers that rolled on the floor, all the shady stuff that Darryl pulled, including the final trip that had something to do with crystal meth, the Winnebago that lumbered over the centre line with Darryl half-dazed, the old guy at the wheel, all that momentum they both built up when they hit. The front grill of the Winnebago went straight head-on through Darryl's rusted-up Chevrolet and it took the motor of that car, in one big jangled piece, slam-back through that smirk of his, and right through Florence too, until they all ended up in the trunk, fused and welded together by the flames that broke out, probably from the cigarette that Darryl always had to have, hanging there from his lip.

That's how Eunice inherited her baby from her sister Flo by accident. Flo had come by earlier that day and left Queenie with her, like she'd had some kind of premonition. She was a good mother, really when you got down to it. "Here," Flo said, "take Queenie a bit. Darryl and me, we're off to where there's no place for a girl." You really can't get much better than that, when it comes to mothering.

RESPITE

On Saturday evenings the writer named Womack takes a break from his novel and looks after the boy. He goes to the boy's house in the suburbs, far from where Womack lives among the other writers and artists in the city. It is winter and he rides out to the suburbs on his bicycle, wheels up slickly in the slush on the street and chains his bicycle to the fence that pens in the yard, then comes into the house, shivering and wet.

The boy is twelve, and dying of a degenerative illness. He can no longer see, hear, walk, or speak, although there are times when he laughs. This laugh is a crackle, a shriek. If Womack were to describe the laugh in his novel it would become *a sudden bolt of blue lightning over an empty, black sea*. Womack is a writer of prose, but fancies himself something of a poet, also. Womack has studied writing in university and wants his novel to be something new, something fresh, and free of cliché; these days he hears cliché even in speech and cringes.

Saturdays are the same, almost without variation: Womack arrives and the boy's mother, Sylvia, is waiting in the living room, standing over her son in his wheelchair. She offers thanks and passes the boy off to Womack and disappears into her bedroom, and Womack then hoists the boy out of his wheelchair and props him up against his body and carries him around the house, and the boy moans. The boy moans and moves his legs as if he were walking, but he is not; the boy's legs hang limply from his body, dragging on the floor. Like this Womack manoeuvres the boy, slowly, step, step, step, from room to room around the house.

The writer Womack used to live with a woman named Adriane whom he had that autumn begun to introduce to people as his partner, as though they were business associates or cops. The word arrived into his vocabulary at a party that was both Halloween party and stag-and-doe party for friends of Womack's, friends named Mike and Cheryl who would be married a week before Christmas. Greeting them in the hallway, Womack's arm draped over Adriane's shoulder, a woman dressed as Fidel Castro introduced another woman, also dressed as Fidel Castro, as her partner, and Womack repeated the word in reference to Adriane. At this, like a child escaping the embrace of a foul-breathed and bearded aunt, Adriane slid out from underneath his arm, nodded at the Castros, and sipped her drink. Later, she confronted him in the kitchen.

Partner? she asked. The kimono of her Geisha outfit shimmered and swished.

Sure, Womack told her. His costume was Hockey Player: helmet, gloves, stick. That's what people say now, he said.

Straight people?

Sure.

For the rest of the evening, Adriane adopted a Texan accent when addressing Womack – Yee-haw! Fetch me another drink, Pardner! Even so, the new label made Womack feel modern and serious. Gone was the term *girlfriend*, used for those who had filled that role since his early teens. Now he had a partner. This was heavy stuff.

At midnight Womack and Adriane came home to the place that they had moved into together that July, their place that was not quite loft and not quite studio, their place where a wall divided two long, high-ceilinged rooms in defiance of architectural categorization. You entered the apartment into a kitchen and dining space; through an arched doorway was a living area with a couch and a stereo and the desk with the computer where Womack wrote his novel. At the back of the room, behind drawn curtains, sat their bed. This area they called The Bedroom, even though it was not technically a room at all.

Adriane, who worked the next day, went straight to bed. Womack ditched the helmet, gloves, and stick in a closet, sat down at his desk in his uncomfortable chair, turned on his computer, and began typing. The uncomfortable chair had wheels and the floor was warped, slightly. At one point, when Womack's typing relented and he let go of the keyboard, the desk released him gliding into the room until he stopped with a bump against the window on the far wall.

Sitting there under the window, the computer glowing across the room, he could hear Adriane's breathing from behind the curtains. This is what their weekdays had become:

dinner or the occasional outing, Adriane falling asleep hours before him, then up early the next morning and off to the counselling centre. Womack would sleep until noon, get up, drink too much coffee, and eventually make it to the computer, to his novel.

In the summer, when they had moved in together, they had bought tropical house plants and named them: Hangy, the bushy one dangling from the ceiling above the dining table; Jules Fern, whose leafy tendrils spread out over the couch; and, guarding the bedroom, sombre and violet: Jacques Laplante. Back then, Adriane would arrive home and it would be sex, first thing, almost before she was even in the door. Her clothes would come off and so would Womack's and they would romp for a while on the bed, if they made it that far, and afterwards have a nice meal wearing only housecoats and slippers. Then there might be more sex and snacks made in the toaster oven, gobbled dripping cheese over the sink, and finally, clinging to one another in bed, Goodnight Adriane, I love you, and, Goodnight Womack, me too, and Adriane would go in bleary-eyed to work the next morning.

Now, this, every night: Womack wide awake at his computer and Adriane asleep behind the curtains. This was the life of couples, he assumed, of partners – functional, pragmatic, a pattern established and repeated with someone who found it mutually tolerable. Womack thought of his parents, marching together through their marriage like soldiers in a military parade. Partners. Life.

But Womack was writing a novel, and he was doing good work. He had written over one hundred pages. The words were coming. Sentences spilled into paragraphs spilled into chapters, while on the periphery Adriane came in and out of the apartment like the mechanical bird in a wind-up clock.

At the house where Womack volunteers there are two other children, the boy's sister and brother: Jessica and Andrew. They are younger, nine and six, and often play the Game of Life on the living room floor while Womack carries their dying older brother around nearby. Womack and the boy step over the two children and their board game, which it seems only Jessica understands and wins convincingly every time, and Womack says, Excuse us, and watches as Jessica takes advantage of the distraction to steal three five-hundred dollar bills and a husband from the box. Nice characterization, notes Womack.

One cold evening a week into November, Adriane came home from yoga class, which she had recently taken up and went to twice a week straight from work. Womack was at the stove, making dinner. Outside, the first snow of the season came sifting down like wet flour from the clouds. It lit briefly on the streets before melting into the grey puddle that soaked the city.

Adriane hung her coat and came into the kitchen. Through the doorway to the other room drifted the sound of the stereo in the next room, playing music. Ah, there's a good Womack, she said, nodding. My little housewife. Her face was pink; icy droplets had collected in her hair and eyelashes.

Womack laughed, stirring a creamy sauce. How were The Youth today?

The Youth were troubled, said Adriane. She pulled the Dictaphone she used for interviews from her pocket, placed it on the kitchen table.

Any good stories?

Adriane snorted, shaking her head. This again, she said.

Oh, come on, said Womack. Who am I going to tell?

Adriane started rifling through the stack of mail on the dining table. Hangy drooped down from above, lush and green. What did you do all day?

What do you think?

She fingered Hangy's foliage. Did you water the plants?

I watered them like a week ago. They're fine.

And the R.S.V.P. to Mike and Cheryl about the wedding?

Oh, come on, Ade. They know we're coming.

She held up an envelope. How about the phone bill?

Oh, shoot. Womack stopped stirring.

Adriane looked up. You're kidding, right?

I got busy.

Busy doing what? You were home all day!

Home, working. The spoon stood erect in the coagulating sauce. It's not like I'm just sitting around and picking my ass.

I guess if you ever called anyone, you'd probably care if the phone got disconnected.

Was this a fight? wondered Womack. Were they fighting?

Adriane looked at him, the look of an executive evaluating an employee at a time of cutbacks and lay-offs. Womack wore the cut-off sweatpants and T-shirt he had gone to bed in the night before. Adriane reached out and pocketed the Dictaphone, then spoke before he could: When was the last time you went outside?

Two nights ago. I picked up sushi, remember?

During the day. For more than errands.

Ade, this is what I do. I'm writing a book.

A novel, she corrected him, smirking.

You go to work with The Youth, I work at home. Okay?

Adriane said nothing. Womack returned to his sauce, which had developed a rubbery skin he now began to churn back in. After a minute, Adriane stood, moved to the front door and put on her coat.

Where are you going? asked Womack.

To the ATM, said Adriane. She held up the envelope. To pay the phone bill.

What the boy likes is doors. He and Womack stop in front of a closed door in the house, a bedroom or a closet, and the boy takes Womack's hand in his and places it on the doorknob, and Womack opens the door and the boy laughs. When Womack closes the door the boy moans and takes Womack's hand again and places it on the doorknob, and this continues until the boy becomes restless, and then they move to a new door in the house. Womack watches the boy delight in the doors and thinks to himself, I should be able to use this as a metaphor for something.

A few days later, Adriane came home from yoga and Womack was wearing a shirt and tie. Dinner was on the table: meatloaf and green beans and rice. She disappeared into the living room, turned off the music that was playing, then reemerged in the kitchen.

What's the occasion? asked Adriane. You look like a dad.

No occasion, said Womack. But thank you.

They sat and ate.

How was yoga? he asked.

Good. You should come sometime.

Ha! Womack nearly choked on a green bean. Yoga! God, like one of those new-age creeps in a unitard and a ponytail, some white guy named Starfire or Ravi. No thanks.

Adriane looked at him, opened her mouth to say something, but seemed to reconsider and instead filled it with meatloaf.

I've been thinking, said Womack, chewing.

Oh, yeah?

Yeah. I've been thinking about maybe volunteering somewhere. You know, getting out and doing something, getting involved. In the community. With people.

Adriane took a sip of water, put the glass back down, waited.

Maybe something with kids, Womack said.

That's a great idea, said Adriane. Womack detected something in her voice, though: hesitancy, maybe. Doubt?

After dinner, Adriane washed the dishes while Womack retreated to his computer. He took off his tie and typed and deleted and typed some more. Adriane did paperwork at the dining table, the murmur of voices playing from the Dictaphone as she made her transcriptions. Eventually she came into the living room, rubbing her eyes, tape recorder in hand.

I'm pooped, she told Womack. Stood there while he stared at the computer screen.

He looked up. Sure, he said. I'm just going to finish this bit, okay?

Adriane turned and disappeared between the curtains. Womack could hear the whisper of clothes coming off and pajamas going on. And then the bedroom light clicking off and the bedside lamp clicking on. He typed these two sentences into his computer.

I'll come kiss you goodnight, Womack called, cutting and pasting the pajama line into another section of his novel. Let me know when you're in bed.

Another click, extinguishing the glow of the bedside lamp. The rustle of sheets. A pillow being fluffed. Silence.

Womack read the section over, then pushed away from the desk on his wheelie chair. Behind the curtains, Adriane lay in bed with her back to him, facing the wall. Womack slid under the covers and put a hand on her back. He felt a tremor in her body. She was masturbating.

Mind if I join you? asked Womack.

Suit yourself, said Adriane, her hand at work between her legs.

Womack reached into his pants and began to coax himself into arousal. Beside him, Adriane's breath came in gasps. After a few minutes, just as Womack was growing hard, she went limp.

Did you finish? he asked.

I'm tired, she said.

Oh.

Outside the snow had become the hiss of light rain.

Okay, said Womack. Sure. Well, goodnight. He leaned in and planted a kiss on the back of Adriane's head. She tensed, slightly.

Everything all right? he asked.

I'm tired, Womack.

Womack lay there, propped up on one elbow, staring at Adriane's back. Eventually, he got up, ducked between the curtains and sat back down at his computer. He typed VOLUNTEERING into an internet search and, with a licorice-scented marker and a stack of Post-It notes, began taking stock of his options.

After an hour or so of Womack carrying the boy around the house, it is time for the boy's supper. This supper is puréed, and usually cauliflower. Sylvia emerges from the bedroom looking half-asleep, heats up the boy's supper in a microwave, and gives it to Womack to feed to her son. At this time she also gets out some leftovers from the week and heats them on the stove for herself and Jessica and Andrew. When everything is ready, everyone sits down at the table: mother and children at one end, Womack and the boy at the other.

A week after submitting his online application, Womack was registered with The Fountain Group, an organization that paired its volunteers with families in need of respite care. The family assigned to Womack was named Dunn; their address was included, and a telephone number if Womack wished to call and introduce himself before he visited their home. He did not.

His first Saturday, Womack woke up early. Adriane was sleeping in; it was her day off. Although Womack was not scheduled to be out at the family's home until four that afternoon, he paced around the apartment, wondering what to wear, eating breakfast, then brunch, then a giant toasted sandwich at a few minutes past noon. He felt nauseous and bloated. It was the first day he had not turned his computer on in months.

From Womack's apartment to the family's house took just under a half hour by bicycle. He rode along the major avenues and boulevards of the city that narrowed into the thin, tree-lined streets of the suburbs. The trees were leafless. The streets were black with melted snow. Eventually Womack pulled up to an address that matched the one on a Post-It note that smelled vaguely of licorice. The family's house was a squat bungalow with a cracked driveway and a lawn littered with children's toys: Tonka trucks and hula-hoops and a few upended sandpails.

Inside, Womack met first Sylvia, then Jessica and Andrew, who both stared for a moment at Womack's outstretched hand before bounding off giggling down the hallway – and then, finally, sitting in the kitchen in his wheelchair and moaning, the boy. Womack approached him as one might a lion escaped from its cage: at a crouch, whispering. Sylvia stood behind the chair and secured the boy's head in an upright position. Saliva dribbled from the corner of his mouth, strung to his shoulder in gooey threads. The boy's eyes were milky and gazed blankly in the direction of, but not at, Womack.

Hello, whispered Womack.

The boy moaned.

He likes to have his face touched, said the boy's mother. She cupped his ears, demonstrating. The boy laughed, a sudden burst like the crack of a cannon. Womack jumped. He composed himself, squatted beside the boy in his wheelchair and, looking up at the mother, replaced her hands with his own. The boy shook his head free, and moaned. Womack stood.

He just needs to get to know you, explained Sylvia.

The rest of the evening Womack spent at a distance observing the boy's routine: Sylvia fed her son, bathed him, eventually put him to bed. He admired her ease with the boy, the mechanical, almost instinctive acts of jeans being pulled off and a diaper being folded on, pajamas, and then the tenderness of her leaning over and stroking his face while he lay in bed and Womack stood in the doorway, dimming the lights. Motherhood, noted Womack. In the front hall, handing Womack his coat, she told him the following week he would be on his own, and did he feel comfortable doing it all himself?

Womack said, Sure, nodding a bit too vigorously.

When Womack got home, Adriane sat at the kitchen table before an offering of Styrofoam tubs. The Dictaphone sat nearby atop a pile of manila folders. She was reading a book – a travel guide: *Southeast Asia on a Shoestring*.

Planning a trip? Womack asked, taking his place at the table.

I wish. Adriane stood and began peeling lids off containers, revealing noodles and stir-fried vegetables, barbecue pork, and cashew chicken. Sitting back down, she added, I mean, I wish I could afford it.

Sure.

Anyway, I ordered Chinese. She gestured at the food. I didn't feel like cooking.

Fair enough, said Womack. He pulled apart a pair of chopsticks. Looks good.

While they ate, Womack detailed his afternoon spent with the boy. Adriane responded with single words muffled by mouthfuls of food: Yeah? Really? Uh-huh.

He's more . . . he's sicker than I thought he would be. Like, he can't really do anything for himself. It'll be me doing pretty much everything – feeding him, giving him a bath. Changing his diaper.

Adriane looked up. Like his mother does every other day?

Oh, she's amazing. Can you imagine? You should see her with him.

Womack didn't know what else to say. What were the words for this? He could only think of clichés – *the power of the human spirit*, stuff like that. Adriane went back to her meal, chopsticks gathering, plucking. They ate silently, methodically, and when the Styrofoam containers had been emptied, Womack put down his chopsticks and looked across the table at Adriane, this woman he had lived with for five months, his partner. She was leaning over the last few scraps of chow mein, eyes on her travel guide.

So, he said, crumpling the empty food containers one by one under his palm, like a tough guy with beer cans. Southeast Asia.

Yep, she said.

Sounds fun.

Adriane speared a piece of pork with her chopstick, lifted it up, bit down, and sucked the meat into her mouth. Something to read, she said.

Just something to read?

Sure. She rolled her eyes. God, listen to me – *sure* – I'm starting to even talk the same as you.

Womack ignored this. Well, why not the newspaper? Why not a book? I've got lots of books. He could hear the crescendo of his own voice. You want to borrow a book?

A *novel*?

Womack paused. When he spoke, his tone was quiet, low, but something uneasy rippled through his voice: What, exactly, is that supposed to mean?

Oh, you know, big writer. You and your *novel*. She slurped a noodle into her mouth. It whacked against her cheek on the way in, leaving a brown stripe across her face. Am I in there? Is there a bitchy girlfriend character? Is she always nagging the hero to take out the garbage and pay the bills?

Since when do you care about my writing? said Womack, aware, immediately, of his own earnestness.

Adriane stared at him, chewing. The saucy stripe lay like a wound across her cheek. *Since when do you care about my writing*, she mimicked, standing, carrying her plate behind the kitchen counter, where she slid it among the dirty dishes piled in the sink. This is my day off, she told him. I have to deal with bullshit all week. I want to have my weekends to relax, not get into these stupid arguments about nothing.

Womack looked away. On the table before him, splayed open to a page titled, When to Go, sat the travel guide. Womack imagined Adriane surfing on a ratty shoelace along the river from *Apocalypse Now*, heads on spikes lining the shores, bullets whizzing through the air. All around, crumpled Styrofoam tubs sat like ruined sandcastles. Womack placed his hands over his ears, tightly. There was a dull echo inside his skull: the empty, hollow rumble of a stalled train.

Feeding the boy is easy; he eats mechanically, unquestioningly. Womack sits the boy in his wheelchair and scoops spoonfuls of puréed food into the boy's mouth, and the boy swallows. At the opposite end of the table sit the boy's mother

and brother and sister with their plates of leftovers, but they
are in a different world, apart. While Womack feeds the boy,
Andrew shovels mashed potatoes and corn at his face, spilling
most of it on the floor; Jessica eats demurely, telling stories
about which boys at school she dislikes this week; Sylvia takes
it all in, nodding, smiling, pushing her food around, hardly
eating. Womack feels invisible, as if he were watching their
meal through a two-way mirror – collecting evidence for a
trial, a detective, or a spy.

In the middle of December Womack surprised Adriane with
dinner reservations at a Vietnamese restaurant. Adriane
smiled at this. Encouraged, Womack kissed her on the cheek,
and took her hand in his as they walked down the street.

At the restaurant, a woman in a Santa hat seated them at a
table for two and handed over menus they struggled to read in
the dim light. Womack, squinting, made a few suggestions –
What about number twenty-three? Or sixteen, the shrimp? –
before the waitress arrived and Adriane ordered a bowl of soup.

Soup? said Womack. He looked apologetically to the waitress. Why don't we share a couple things?

I'm not that hungry, said Adriane. She gazed around the
restaurant, up at the walls decorated with posters and maps of
Vietnam, at the shelves of ornaments by the door. A few
booths over, a couple were drinking with their arms entwined.

Womack decided on the shrimp dish for himself, plus a
half-litre of house wine for the two of them, to share.

The waitress left, smiling. Womack looked at Adriane,
then over at the romancing couple, then back at her. He
rolled his eyes.

What's wrong with that? she asked, staring back.

Nothing, said Womack. Just a little cheesy.

They were silent until the food and wine arrived, and even then, their meal was only punctuated by Womack asking, How's your soup? to which Adriane responded, Good, how's your shrimp? to which Womack responded, Good, and then Adriane slurped her soup and Womack chewed his shrimp, which were not good at all, but overcooked and rubbery, and when the meal was over Adriane put it on her Visa and they left the restaurant and walked home, Womack behind Adriane, single-file.

Back in the apartment Adriane went directly to bed, and Womack, tipsy from the half-litre of house wine he'd drunk alone, sat at his desk with the computer monitor off, staring at the blank screen.

When he is full, the boy moans. Womack excuses himself from the table with the boy's dishes, rinses them in the sink, stacks them in the dishwasher, and then wheels the boy into his bedroom, where they sit for a while. Womack sits on the bed and tells the boy, You need to digest your food. The boy moans and rocks slightly in his wheelchair. Womack looks out the window of the boy's room, at the sun setting or the children's swingset in the backyard, and thinks about the novel he is writing. He has wanted for some time for this boy to become a character – someone tragic, his novel lacks pathos – but how to write about a dying child without resorting to sentimentality, to cliché?

That Thursday, two days before Mike and Cheryl's wedding, Adriane announced to Womack that she would only be able to make it to the reception.

There's this Hot Yoga class starting on Saturday afternoons, she told him over a dinner of fish sticks and peas. If I don't go to the first one, they won't let me sign up.

Hot Yoga? said Womack, stabbing at a single pea with his fork. Ade, these are two of my best friends.

Really? When was the last time you talked to them? Halloween?

Whoa, said Womack. The pea rolled away; he put down his fork.

I'll be there for the reception – that's what matters. They won't even notice me missing at the ceremony. And you know how I feel about church and religion and all that.

I've cancelled volunteering for the day, Ade. You don't think you could just do your Hot Yoga some other time? He looked at her. What the fuck is Hot Yoga, anyway?

Sorry, she said, and reached across the table, unexpectedly, to squeeze Womack's hand. He felt something like warmth at this contact, and hated himself for that.

At the wedding ceremony Womack sat at the end of a pew in the back of the church, the space beside him conspicuously empty. When Cheryl came up the aisle he turned with everyone else, beaming, trying to catch her eye. She stared ahead, some strange mix of terror and joy on her face, and walked deliberately down the middle of the congregation as though she were trying to ignore everyone there.

After the vows and photos and everything else, and the two hundred-person congregation had shifted to the community centre across town, Womack found his seat at a table with strangers, right near the front of the reception hall. The folded card on his plate read *Womack + Guest*. The room began to fill, and Womack kept asking the woman on the other side of the empty chair between them what time it was, before, finally, just as the head groomsman was about to give his speech, Adriane came breezing in. She was dressed in black pants and a black sweater, and her hair was still wet from the shower.

Thanks for showing up, whispered Womack as she sat down.

Adriane shook out her napkin and laid it across her lap. That was some *hot* yoga.

Right, said Womack, and pulled away.

The speeches began. They were long. Adriane sat there, her back to the stage, staring into space. Womack drank a few glasses of wine and began to feel disappointed that he hadn't been asked to speak. He would have been good. He was a writer, for fuck's sake.

Then the speeches were over and Cheryl was standing up at the front with a big white bouquet, facing backward, and a cluster of women were gathered jostling at the front of the hall. The DJ got on the microphone and everyone joined in the countdown, and at Zero! Cheryl launched the bouquet upwards over her head, and even before it landed, Womack could trace the trajectory, could see in horror that it was coming toward his table. When it smacked down on Adriane's plate he could only stare into all those flowers, the ivory gloss of them. He was aware vaguely of Adriane saying something like, Oh, fucking fantastic, and felt nothing when they got home later and her first move was to the kitchen, where she stuffed the entire bouquet into the trash underneath the sink.

After the boy digests dinner it is time for his bath, and Womack fills the tub and strips the boy down and lifts him up and eases him into the water, which Womack takes great care to ensure is the right temperature. The water sloshes around and Womack struggles for a simile to describe it to himself in his head, but the boy is floundering about in the water and needs calming, so Womack abandons similes and instead attempts to soothe the boy by putting his hands over the boy's ears. The boy's thrashing subsides; he sinks down into the water with Womack's hands on his face, smiling, laughing. Then Womack sponges the boy down and shampoos his hair, and when the boy is pink and rosy and clean, Womack lifts him out of the tub and towels him off.

It was just over two weeks until Christmas, and Womack decided to buy a turkey. At the supermarket he scooped one from the deep-freeze and brought it home on his bicycle in his backpack. When Adriane came home that evening from yoga, after she turned off his music and reappeared in the kitchen, Womack opened up the refrigerator door and displayed it to her, proudly, as if it were something he himself had constructed or laid.

Better keep it in the freezer, said Adriane.

Yeah?

Well, it's not going to keep in there forever.

Doesn't it look delicious?

Adriane eyed the turkey, a pinkish lump nestled between the milk and pickles. It looks like a dead bird, she said.

Womack slammed the fridge door. For fuck's sake, Ade.

What? She was laughing at him.

Can you get excited about anything?

A turkey? You want me to get excited about a turkey?

Well, something.

Adriane shook her head and went into the living room. Womack followed her and stood in the doorway, watching her remove the Dictaphone from her pocket, place it softly on the coffee table, then pick up *Southeast Asia on a Shoestring*, and start reading.

So when are we going? he asked.

Adriane laughed, turning the page. You think you could afford it?

Womack faltered. He could feel what was coming, knew it from so many bad TV shows, the script of The Couple's Fight.

What is this? he asked her, finally.

What is what?

This. You. Never home. And when you are, acting like I don't exist – not talking, disappearing into that book, going to bed.

Don't you ever get tired of just sitting around? There was something tired and pleading in Adriane's eyes. Womack did his best not to read it as pity.

You want to take a vacation? he demanded. Take a vacation. Go. I'm not stopping you. I'll lend you an extra shoestring, if you want.

Oh, put it in your novel, writer. Adriane sighed, closed the book, and flopped back on the couch. She was silent. Womack was silent. Then there was a loud click from the Dictaphone. They both looked down at it sitting almost guiltily on the coffee table.

What the hell? he asked, moving across the room.

Adriane stood. Don't, she said.

But Womack was already there, the recorder in his hand,

hitting the EJECT button, popping the cassette out of the recorder. What's this? You're taping our conversations?

Adriane was reaching toward him, a nervous expression on her face.

Give that to me.

Womack slid the cassette back into the Dictaphone, hit REWIND for a few seconds, then PLAY.

From the speaker, his own voice, tinny, but audible: *Can you get excited about anything?*

And then Adriane's: *A turkey? You want me to get excited about a turkey?*

His, more incredulous and desperate than he remembered: *Well, something.*

And so on, their voices, back and forth. Finally, Adriane's, *Oh, put it in your nov* – was cut off, and the tape began to whine before snapping to a stop.

Womack stood for a moment, silent, gazing at the Dictaphone in his hand as if it might speak up and offer an explanation. Adriane sat down on the couch.

How long have you been doing this? Womack asked, his back to her.

Adriane said nothing.

He rewound the cassette, further this time, letting the counter wind backward a few hundred digits. He pressed PLAY.

Here he was: *I guess so, yeah.* This was followed by hiss, the odd clank of something metallic. Chewing. Womack watched the wheels of the cassette turn, waiting. Then, himself again: *So, Southeast Asia.*

Yep, she said.

Sounds fun.

A pause. Her: *Something to read.*

Just something to read?

Womack hit STOP. Christ, he said. You're messed up, you know that? He took the cassette out of the recorder, turned it over in his hands.

There was a sigh from the couch, but Womack refused to look over. He wiggled his finger into the empty space at the base of the cassette, hooked it under the tape, and began pulling, pulling – not angrily, but purposefully, the wheels spinning, however many of their recorded arguments unravelling into piles of glistening black ribbon at his feet.

After bathing the boy, Womack has to get a diaper on him, which is always a struggle. With one hand Womack lifts the boy's legs and holds them together at the ankles, knees bent, while with the other he hoists up the boy's backside and attempts to wedge the diaper underneath. Occasionally the diaper ends up going on the wrong way, but by then Womack is often so exhausted he says, Fuck it, to himself, and pulls the boy's pajamas on over the backwards diaper, and gives him some pills. The boy might at this point again be moaning. Womack does the hands-on-the-ears thing. It has become a reflex. The boy grins, gurgling, cooing. With his hands cupped over the boy's ears, Womack looks down at him, at the boy lying on the bed in his pajamas, something like delight on his face, and he tries not to think the expected thoughts of fortune and misfortune, chance and fate.

Two nights after the incident with the recorder, Womack and Adriane had another argument that, with Adriane in bed and him sitting before his computer, filled Womack with shame and embarrassment. He recalled himself screaming things like, Will you think of someone other than yourself, for once? and Adriane crying and screaming back, When was the last time we did anything fun?

As Womack sat there, from behind the curtains in The Bedroom came the light whistle of a snore, the creak of bedsprings as Adriane turned in her sleep. Womack pictured her, wrapped in the covers – but the image included him, lying next to her, staring into her face as she slept. A hard knot rose in his throat. Womack sighed deeply, rose from the uncomfortable chair, pushed through the curtains, and stood looking down at Adriane, her eyes closed, mouth half-open, hair splayed across the pillow.

Hey, he said.

A pasty, smacking sound from her mouth.

He sat down on the bed, reached out, and prodded her with his fingertips. Hey.

Adriane rolled over. What time is it?

Ade, this isn't right. Us sleeping in the same bed.

What? She sat up.

Us, like this. I can't do it, act like nothing's wrong, lie down next to you. I can't sleep like that. Like, physically, I can't sleep.

Okay?

So maybe one of us should sleep on the couch. Like we could take turns, or whatever.

Look at you, she said. Her mouth was a crescent-shaped shadow in the dark.

Me?

Making decisions. I'm impressed.

What are you talking about?

I'm talking about you, actually doing something for a change. Not just sitting back and watching and then going to your computer and typing it all down.

I'm sorry?

You know, it's too bad you wrecked that tape I was making. I was planning on playing it back for you, so you could actually hear yourself. Like, for real, instead of the version you make up in your head.

What would you know about that?

Listen, she said, kicking the covers off. I think one of us sleeping on the couch is a great idea. And I volunteer myself. Seriously. No problem. The bed's all yours.

And then she ducked through the curtains and was gone. Womack looked down at the S-shaped indentation her body had imprinted on the mattress. Lying down, curling his own body to fill the shape, he could smell Adriane's hair on the pillow. He pulled the sheets around him and cocooned himself within the heat she had left behind.

Womack's last task before he puts the boy to bed is to give him water. This is not as simple as running the tap into a cup and tipping it down the boy's throat; while puréed foods are not a problem, the boy chokes on liquids. Drinking is a complicated, almost medical procedure. The boy has been outfitted with a sort of valve above his bellybutton. It looks to Womack like a valve you might find on a pair of children's water-wings: a little tube that juts out of the boy's stomach, and a stopper on a flexible hinge that plugs and unplugs the opening of the tube. In the corner of the bedroom, Womack sits the boy down in his wheelchair, lifts his shirt to expose the valve, and attaches a tube connected to an IV bag hanging from the ceiling. Water from the bag drips along the tube and directly into the boy's stomach. Womack sits back, waiting, and watches the boy drink.

One of the last nights before Adriane moved out, Womack came home from volunteering and she was sleeping in the bed, the curtains open. The blankets on the couch were still there, crumpled in a woolly ball from where she had kicked them that morning. It was early, barely nine o'clock. Womack stood between the open curtains, looking down on her lying there, listening for the whistle of her breath. There was silence. Womack knew she was awake.

Hey, he said, getting into bed.

There was no reply, but Womack could feel her shifting, moving closer.

Hey, he said, again.

Adriane turned over. Womack reached out and put his hand to her face, felt the wetness of tears on her cheek.

Just sleeping, right? said Adriane. No fooling around.

Womack nodded, avoided saying anything about old time's sake.

He slid one arm underneath her neck, another around her back, his thigh between her legs. Their faces were close. Her breath was salty and hot. I miss you, he said.

Adriane sniffed.

He kissed her, then, but the kiss felt only like a gesture: a handshake, a nod, a wave goodbye. Then she turned and he curled tightly into her back and closed his eyes. After a few minutes like this, he felt her body relax as she fell asleep. Her breath came in deep, restful sighs.

Womack lay there, the tickle of Adriane's hair against his face. Sleepless minutes became an hour. An hour became two. He was hot. He kicked the covers off. Another hour passed. Womack thought, Sleep, sleep, to himself. He tried to match his breathing to hers. Eventually, he rolled away, releasing her and sat up. Legs dangling off the bed, Womack looked at Adriane over his shoulder. Her face.

In the kitchen Womack filled a mug with milk and put it in the microwave, which whirred to life and cast a yellow glow into the dark kitchen. He leaned back on the counter in front of the refrigerator, smiled, then reached forward, opening the freezer. A cold blast of air, and there was the turkey, surrounded by ice cube trays and TV dinners and Tupperware.

In the living room, Womack sat down with his warm milk on the uncomfortable chair and turned on his computer. He sipped at the milk while things booted up, thinking of the turkey in the freezer: a last sad attempt at domesticity, futile and abandoned and collecting the white fur of frost.

When the computer was ready, he opened up the file on the desktop that was his novel and sat there, reading it over, rolling slightly this way and that. He leaned back. The milk was done. He let the cup rest in his lap, stretched out his legs, and the next morning when Adriane woke, she found him asleep in the chair underneath the window, the computer's screensaver whirling around on the other side of the room.

On the boy's bed are a harness and guardrail to prevent him from rolling out over the course of the night. These Womack once forgot to put in place; he realized the following morning and promptly called the boy's mother to make sure the boy had not cracked his skull open over the course of the night. The boy had not. Sylvia explained that every night after Womack leaves the house, she checks on her son and kisses him goodnight.

Now it is the last Saturday before Christmas. Next week the family has told Womack to take the day off. A holiday. But today Womack is scheduled to head out there on his bicycle, to go through his routine with the boy of opening doors and supper and bathtime and bedtime.

In his place that he now inhabits alone, in his place that is not quite loft and not quite apartment, his place that contains just under half as much furniture and two less tropical house plants than it did a few weeks prior, Womack gets ready for his day of volunteering. He eats a sensible lunch of a bowl of soup, a bagel, and an apple. The coffee maker is gone, so instead Womack makes a cup of tea, which he sips while he edits a draft of his novel, not yet complete but still printed out and lying in two stacks on the kitchen table. He works with a blue pen on the stack of paper to his right. The completed pages he turns over and adds to the stack to his left. If he is honest with himself, he would admit that he cannot write anything new; the editing gives him something to do.

When it is time to leave, Womack finishes the page he is working on, stands, puts on his coat and hat and gloves, checks for the key to his bike lock in his pocket. At the door on his way out, he pauses for a moment, looking back across the kitchen, at the refrigerator, at the freezer.

At the family's house Sylvia is waiting, as always, with her son in his wheelchair, but this time the other children are decorating a Christmas tree in the corner of the room. Andrew is hanging ornaments with methodical symmetry; Jessica is wrapping the branches in silver tinsel. A blue macaroni angel looms above. Womack removes his coat and hat and gloves, lowers his backpack to the ground.

What's in the bag? asks the boy's mother.

Ah, says Womack. A little present.

He opens the zipper, and, shaking the backpack a bit, produces the turkey.

A turkey, says Sylvia. Beside her, the boy begins to moan.

I thought we could maybe have it tonight, says Womack, cradling it like an infant, adding, Together.

That's very kind of you, says Sylvia, but I think it's still frozen. It'll take at least a day to thaw before we can even think about cooking it.

Womack wavers at this, feeling vulnerable and foolish.

Hastily, Sylvia holds out her hands for the turkey. But if you're not going to eat it, we'd love to keep it for another time.

Womack smiles. The boy moans. Okay, says Womack.

The rest of the afternoon is spent predictably: the walking about, the doors, supper, the boy's bath. Womack lies the boy down on his bed, lifts the boy's legs up in the air, does his best to get the diaper on. Next: pajamas. Outside the December sky glows a dull orange. Womack closes the blinds of the boy's bedroom, pulls back the covers, starts to lift the latches on the guardrail to secure it alongside the mattress.

When the boy is safely in bed, Womack's duties will be over for the evening. He will cross the hall and knock on Sylvia's bedroom door. He will hear the click of the lock and the door will open and Sylvia will smile a tired sort of smile and say, Thank you, Martin, Merry Christmas, and Martin Womack will say, No problem, Merry Christmas to you too. He will say, See you in two weeks, Sylvia, and Sylvia will say, Yes.

But tonight, Womack realizes, in the living room Jessica and Andrew will not be packing up the Game of Life, Jessica having won again, her little car packed with the blue and pink pegs of a successful family, her bank account bursting, her assets bountiful. They will have finished decorating the tree. They might be watching a movie, a Christmas movie, the tree blinking coloured lights from the corner of the room. Goodbye, Womack will whisper, as he puts on his coat. Jessica will say, Your turkey's in the fridge, not turning from the movie, and Andrew will wave and grin.

And so Womack will leave the family. He will head outside and unchain his bicycle and hop up onto it and push off and begin to pedal his way home, where his half-written novel waits for him on his kitchen table. The bicycle will cut down the darkened streets of the suburbs, heading toward the city and the novel. The streets will be black and wet with melted snow and spangled golden with street-lights, and riding back home along them, through the winter night, will tonight feel to Womack a little bit like falling.

JEAN VAN LOON

STARDUST

The Tay River slips without a sound under the low farm
bridge. It tarries, black and slow, among the rushes and
overhanging willows, following the path it has followed for
centuries, a mirror for dragonflies, a steady unchanging home
for rock bass, water snakes, frogs, and the silver-sided fish that
glistens in the sun as it jumps free of a small boy's line. The boy
– fat and orange in a life jacket – stands beside his father, talking
about the bait store and the friend he saw there, whom he
knows from the playground, who was wearing running shoes
with lights built into the heels. Over the trill of a cicada, he talks
about what he and his father will see when they go to the dump.

The bridge is on a private lane that leads from the county
road to the cottage of Franklyn Moore and his family. Even
in the August heat, Franklyn looks neat, his slicked-back hair
damp from a cooling dunk under the tap, a fresh shirt tucked
into his jeans. The sun-baked planks feel hot through
the denim when he sits. He looks back at the route he and

four-year-old Jason walked to get here – the level track across the cow pasture, the steep gravelled climb up the hill behind which the lane dips toward the log cottage, sheltered by a wood that overlooks a small pure lake.

Franklyn keeps a watchful eye on his son. He smiles at the boy's continuous chatter. His eye follows the sinuous shore of the Tay. He's conscious of the irreplaceable joy of this moment, one that he'll recall some day at his computer as he lashes his brain to work faster, or at four in the morning when he wakes – heart racing, muscles keyed – with a sense of something terrible about to swallow him. He'll remember the sweet air, the seeping calm, the young high voice of his son.

Something white moves in the current at the base of a reed bed. Not, as he first thought, the foam of a discarded worm tub. It's luminous as a frog's belly. The anomalous sight pulls him. With one eye on the boy, he stands and saunters across the bridge, onto the shoreline tangled with spotted touch-me-not. His almost new athletic shoes sink among the reeds, and warm water rises to his ankles, releasing a tarry smell. He parts the reeds with his hands.

"Where're you going, Dad?"

A human foot. Small and delicate. It has been severed above the ankle. The cut or the nibbling of fish afterward has created a frill-like border, and scallops of skin move independently in the flow.

He sloshes back to the bridge.

"We have to go now."

"Aw-w-w?!️ We just started." Jason begged all morning to go fishing.

Franklyn picks up the container of worms and jams on the lid. "Pull in your line."

"Why can't we fish?"

Franklyn cannot speak. They cross the pasture in silence. Jason begins to cry. Franklyn picks him up, life jacket, fishing rod, and all, and struggles up the loose footing of the hill, sweat stinging his eyes. He sets the boy down when they reach the tall white pine at the top. Then they walk, hand in hand, down the slope to the parking area and into the cottage.

Marta, Franklyn's wife, has just returned from a swim, dark hair pasted to her head.

"What's wrong?"

"Pack up. We're leaving."

"Why?" Marta asks.

"Jason, go and find me a nice stone." He and the boy have been collecting rocks of different colours and shapes.

"Why?" asks Jason.

"Please find me a stone." Franklyn's voice is hard.

The screen door slaps shut behind the child, and Franklyn explains what he's seen. Marta's towel-draped hand flies to her mouth.

The police arrive within thirty minutes. Franklyn meets them at the bridge. The foot has drifted to the downstream side, but is still visible. While one officer retrieves it, Franklyn answers questions for the other. He answers the same questions for an officer from a second car, and a third. He's there for two hours, policemen three abreast scouring the banks of the river from his lane to the next in both directions.

When he arrives back at the cottage, Marta is still in her

bathing suit. She's taken Jason for a swim, and they're both dripping.

"Mum says we can get running shoes with lights for school."

Marta's eyes are fixed on her husband. "Do they have any idea what's happened?"

"Nothing's packed," says Franklyn.

"Tomorrow could we go to the dump?" asks Jason.

"I don't see the point of running away," says Marta. "Whatever happened was probably far from here. You need – we all need this holiday, and we've just got here."

Franklyn pulls the cooler from under the kitchen counter, opens the fridge, and loads in milk, peanut butter, salad greens, and the steaks he and Marta had planned to grill tonight after Jason went to bed.

"There's no way I could sleep here tonight," he says. His face is taut.

Marta turns. "Come on, Jason. We're going home."

"When we're home can we buy the running shoes?"

They stuff their gear haphazardly into the car.

"I'm sorry," Franklyn says as they drive away from the gate.

Marta looks out the window, avoiding his glance as she's done since she started to pack.

"You didn't see it," Franklyn says.

Marta shields her eyes from the glare as she watches Jason splash in the wading pool at the park. It's Wednesday and there's been no break in the heat. She soaked herself as soon as they came, and her wet bathing suit makes the temperature endurable. Some holiday. Franklyn has gone back to work. As soon as they got home on Sunday, he weeded the garden. Then he washed and waxed the car and vacuumed it inside. After dinner he started to clean the basement.

This is exactly the weather to be in the country. Last night Marta told Franklyn that if he still didn't want to go she'd take Jason to the cottage herself.

"Are you trying to drive me crazy?" said Franklyn. His eyes stared from caves, and the skin on his face looked two sizes too small.

Marta buckles Jason into the back seat of the car. Her forehead drips with sweat. She's headed for IKEA. She hates the crowds there, but it's air-conditioned, and something about the clutter of the store is joyful. It sets off her imagination, and she starts to redecorate in her head, assembling that duvet cover, this chair, that curtain, to transform a bedroom. Not today, she vows. Baskets only. Wicker, in the pale natural colour that makes any space look fresh. Small for the bathroom, medium for toys in the living room, large for next winter's boots in the vestibule.

She pulls out of the driveway and Jason begins to sing.

Baa baa black sheep
Have you any woe.

Wicker baskets saved her marriage, she's told her women friends, a trick she learned from teaching a classroom of six-year-olds. Franklyn used to drive her mad, stopping the minute he walked in the door to pick up every last block, every last plastic truck, his face knotted in a look that said it was her fault.

She finally realized he couldn't help it; he really couldn't tolerate disorder. That's where the baskets came in. Clutter on the dresser? Throw it in a basket. Throw toys in a basket and shove the lot into a corner. Contained chaos is what she aims for. They can both live with that. And she saves on toys. When a friction truck is dumped into a jumble of other toys, it can disappear for weeks. When it turns up again, it's new.

"When we go back to the cottage, can we go to the dump?"

"I don't know." Jason's asked that every day since they came home. He doesn't ask about swimming or fishing or going out in the boat. Just about the dump. Last time, all three of them went, Jason running from pile to pile pointing out the doll with no head, the broken chair, the mattress with the big tear in it that could be a door to an animal's house. Franklyn smiled with Marta as they watched, but he jangled his keys and soon called for them to get back into the car. "Cathartic," he calls a trip to the dump. But he never wants to linger.

It's four-thirty when they get home. Inside, the house is dim. She and Franklyn have resisted air-conditioning – a large expense for the few days each summer when the heat is really excessive. This summer she'd welcome it, though it means sealing up the house the same as in winter. They've been keeping the windows and doors closed anyhow, and the curtains pulled – to conserve the cool of the night as long as possible. She remembers the sealed-in summer gloom of her grandmother's house, dark green blinds pulled low in every window. At least that house had a porch. A screened porch, where you could sit in comfort and watch the world go by. She raises the kitchen blinds, cranks out the casements, and looks into the heavy afternoon. Then she opens the back door and the curtains of the dining room. Then the front door and all the curtains and windows on the second floor. As she stands at the top of the stairs, a breeze lifts the hairs on her arm.

Back in the kitchen, she takes out some small red potatoes. She rinses them under the tap, picks out the few blemishes, and puts them into a saucepan to boil for potato salad. Just as she's about to turn on the stove, Franklyn strides into the kitchen.

"Where have you been?" His voice is sharp.

Marta whirls to confront him. "I've been taking your son to the park, buying baskets to keep things neat because that's what you insist on, and now I'm making dinner for all of us. Any objections?"

"I was trying to phone you and got no answer."

"There were no messages waiting when I got home."

"I called your cell. That's what it's for."

"On a day when it's eighty-seven degrees and humid, I'm not going to weigh my sundress down with a cell phone just so you can reach me at any second. What's wrong with you?"

"What's wrong with wanting to keep in touch?"

"I don't want to be on a leash, that's what. I don't phone you several times a day."

Franklyn throws the *Perth Courier* on the counter, the newspaper of the town closest to their cottage. It's folded to show the picture of a boy.

"I wanted to talk to you about this. They found the torso near the dump."

Marta picks up the paper. As she scans the article, she hears Franklyn click the burner on. She looks up at him.

"I just needed to hear your voice," he says.

She looks up at him. He must know she can't help. She's just another person.

"I've been thinking of taking Jason to visit my mother. We could fly to Moncton tomorrow and come back in ten days. There'd still be time for both of us to get ready for school."

She watches Franklyn's face. He's trying. She can see it in the way he swallows before he speaks, in the way he holds all edge from his voice.

"Maybe I could fly down for the weekend."

He must have seen something in her expression, because he quickly adds, "Not this coming weekend, but the second one. We could fly back together."

It's almost dusk when Franklyn arrives at the gate to the cottage lane. A remnant of yellow police tape hangs from one of the gateposts. It's been hard the past week, but he's done well. He phoned only once a day, and his conversations with Marta were as warm and lively as if nothing were wrong. Jason chattered about his trip to Parlee Beach, his visit to the munic- ipal park, his new running shoes with green lights in the heels. Marta had to pry him from the phone. Franklyn has kept himself busy with rented movies, in the dark of the basement rec room, pulled into sunny worlds of fictional people. The last few nights he hasn't dreamt of the foot.

He shuts the gate behind him, gets back into the car, and drives steadily across the bridge. On the other side of the Tay, he rolls down the windows. The grass is loud with crickets. The tang of the evening pasture mingles with the warm animal smell of a herd of cows that straddles the road. He nudges the car forward. Most of the cattle move to the side. One calf walks a few paces along the track, then stops and turns, chewing its cud, showing neither confidence nor fear. Jason would have loved to see it. Franklyn edges the car closer. The calf walks a bit farther, swings its heavy head around again, blinks its chocolate eyes. At last it ambles off the road and Franklyn proceeds up the hill.

The tall pine still stands by the parking lot. The cottage still smells inside of cedar. He stashes beer in the fridge, and a bagel with cream cheese. He ate a hamburger on the way here, and he's leaving for the airport after breakfast, so he doesn't need much food.

He walks to the living room window that looks down the hillside. Through the trees, under the darkening sky, the lake shines platinum light. The water is glass-still until a tiny flip triggers concentric circles near the dock – no doubt one of the baby bass that Jason likes to look at through his swim mask. Franklyn opens the windows. Usually Marta does that. She goes from room to room, her movements quick and light, her voice spilling in laughter at something she sees from the window. She laughed at the chaos that came with Jason's birth, at the dining-room table used for changing diapers, the floor covered with toys and books and gummed arrowroots. "Surely we could keep a path clear to the kitchen," he had said when he could stand it no more.

When it's fully dark he steps onto the deck. He lies with his back on the bare wood, interlaced fingers pillowing his head, a second beer at his side. The Milky Way is clearly visible – millions of stars swirling in space, a cloud of bright dust. In the city it's easy to forget the scale of the universe, the huge span of time it embraces. A star shoots across the sky, snuffs like a roman candle. This is the week of the Perseids, the newspaper said. Marta would say he gets a wish. All he wants is for his family to be safe.

Tomorrow when he flies to Moncton he'll tell her he's been here. She's right – a freak incident can't be allowed to ruin this place. Despite washouts to the road, failures of the water pump, mosquito infestations in June, the porcupine that gnawed on the main supporting beam, it's where he's felt most at peace. He closes his eyes and listens to the night.

A twig snaps – in the wood that screens their property from the next, he thinks. When the family first spent time here, he checked every sound, looking for a deer or maybe a moose, finding a small red squirrel. Another snap. He props himself on an elbow. There's a glow from next door, visible through drought-shrivelled leaves. Maybe somebody's there for once. A bonfire? There's a ban because everything's so dry. He steps into the living room for binoculars. The light is orange. It flickers. He pats his pocket for his cell phone and picks up a flashlight.

He follows the gravel track to where the woodlot ends, at a field between his lane and the one serving cottages farther along the lake. He climbs the snake-fence into the field, parting the goldenrod that already smells like fall, crunching through dry stalks to the accommodating gap left by a missing log in the opposite fence. He smells smoke. As he climbs the slope leading to the neighbour's gate he hears the rush of burning. The fire is in a shed between him and the cottage, and flames slip over the top of its rough door. There's no car in sight, no sign of occupation. He calls the emergency number, describes how to get to the property, and waits.

He cannot see the propane tank on the other side of the shed. A large tank of the sort used for a refrigerator, a stove and lighting, maybe a fireplace. He doesn't know that the tank is just half full, that the metal above the surface of the liquid has begun to soften in the heat, that in minutes the weakened steel, unequal to its pressurized contents, will blow, and the liquid released will expand nearly three hundred-fold in an orange ball burning at over a thousand degrees.

He turns and starts to walk away. The lane has several forks. He'll meet the fire truck at the gate from the county road.

Jason runs across the floor of the airport waiting room, lights in the heels of his white shoes flashing with each step. He stops with a squeak of rubber on polished aggregate.

Yesterday Franklyn called after lunch. Marta had been dozing on the deck. At the sound of his voice something melted inside her, and she wanted to keep him talking – about the sun-scorched lawn and municipal watering restrictions, about his arrival time and his trouble in booking the flight. She'd fallen in love with his talk. The night they met he drove her home from a party, asking questions, telling stories, keeping the conversation going, building the connections between them as she snatched glances at his profile, at the compact shoulders under his plaid cotton shirt. Today she'll drive him home. She'll hear his breath beside her in the night.

The plane from Montreal has landed, and the first passengers hurry from the gate – people in business clothes, carrying laptops. Returning holidayers spill out next, with shopping bags and backpacks, happy fatigue in their faces. Then a young mother with a two-year-old and a baby, helped by a cabin attendant who unfolds a stroller while the baby wails. And an elderly couple, he with a cane. Then nobody.

"Where's Daddy?"

Marta approaches the desk by the gate.

The attendant types an astonishing number of characters into her keyboard. "There've been delays out of Ottawa," she says at last. "He could have missed the connection in Montreal." She types some more. "Or if he missed the link from Ottawa to Montreal, he might have flown on WestJet via Hamilton. There's a flight coming from there in an hour."

An hour is just the wrong length of time. If it were two, Marta would drive home to her mother's and come back later. If it were half an hour, keeping Jason amused wouldn't be hard. She should have brought her cell phone, so she could ask Franklyn what's happened. He'd say it serves her right she doesn't know.

In the end she decides to wait. She takes Jason to the snack bar and buys him a chocolate milkshake, which looks far too large for a boy his size but which he drains through a straw to the last rattling suck. Then they return to the gate. Jason sits on the edge of the seat and swings his legs, bending to admire the lights. Marta looks from the Arrivals screen to the gate, from the gate to the Arrivals screen. She keeps one hand on her purse and the other on the shoulder of her son, to keep him from running off somewhere and getting lost.

REBECCA ROSENBLUM

CHILLY GIRL

O nce there was a girl who was usually cold. No one liked to hold her hand. She wore toques from October to April. She ruined picnics by wanting to go home when the sun went down. She could cradle lit candles in her bare hands and never get burned.

Once she was seated near a draft at a wedding banquet and her lips turned blue.

Once she forgot to wear a sweater to the movies and her teeth began to chatter.

Once she looked at her cup of tea and then at the man who had bought it for her at a sidewalk café, and said, "I wish I could be *in* a cup of tea right now." He didn't call her again.

Once she got invited to a condo-warming party for her boss. It was July, which made her brave, so she put on her favourite dress, which was yellow and orange and pink. All those gleaming shades of warm, but the fabric was thin cotton. In rain or wind it was as good as being naked. If someone photographed her with a flash, the picture would show an outline of her bra or her sharp little nipples, depending. She took out a cardigan in case of inclement weather or photography and draped it over her arm. Then she went into the living room, where her roommate was watching a noisy Britcom. Her roommate pressed MUTE when the girl came in.

"You're wearing stockings and heels."

"Yes," said the girl. She felt nervous.

"With a sundress. To a summer party."

"It's at Emmy's condo – she's probably got air conditioning."

"You look ridiculous." Her roommate turned the volume back up and watched a lady fall into a pile of grass clippings. She was like that.

The girl slunk back into her room. She kicked off her pumps and peeled her stockings from her legs. She put sandals on her bare feet and tiptoed past her roommate out the door. She was like that.

The party was big but quiet. The girl didn't see an air-conditioning unit but she felt a whispery artificial shiver crawl over her shoulders all the same. She pulled her cardigan on over her summer dress, sad to see her colours disappear. She was fluffing her hair out of the collar when the hostess came darting up to her.

"Oh, *there* you are! I was afraid you wouldn't come."

"I'm happy to have come. It's such a nice place," said the girl.

"Oh, really? Some days, I don't know. Come with me and I'll give you a tour." The hostess took a step and then stopped. Her face flowered up a little. "But . . . could you take off your shoes? I'm sorry, we just had the floors done when we moved in and it was *such* a *thing*. You know. . . ." The hostess looked miserable, like she didn't want to ask but someone had made her.

The girl looked around the living room. There were no shoes anywhere. Hairy pale feet, feet in thin nylon trouser socks, slim feet with pedicures, even stockings . . . no shoes. There could be no exceptions to this rule – someone might get stepped on, delicate naked toes under the grinding hard rubber of a heel.

The girl took off her sandals. The floor felt like icy cement, even though it was parquet. She went on the tour. She put her toes onto the blond parquet squares and walked down halls like Ls and Ts. The kitchen had a butcher's block in the centre covered with dishes of beans and grains. The burners were flush with the stove. The floors gleamed like an ice rink. They walked past high windows where the view pitched into the harbour. If she stood still, the girl could feel some unseen fan blowing the strands of her hair. The hostess glittered at her, the track lighting reflecting shiny and sharp off nails, teeth, eye-whites, tongue. She was lovely and sleek and her home was lovely and sleek and the girl was glad when Emmy finally left her on a couch beside the wet bar, where all her friends were sitting, too.

Her friends were glad to see her, but the people they introduced her to recoiled when they shook her icicle hand. Someone gave her a drink. The ice cubes clinked whenever the girl gestured, or trembled. She was worried her hand would freeze to the glass. She sat on the couch but the creamy beige leather was slippery and glossy and cool against her thighs through the cheap cotton of her dress.

Her friends told her that a woman named Maya, who had caramel hair and used to go out with the girl, was somewhere at the party. The girl stood up. Everyone was concerned. The girl explained that her ex-girlfriend was still her friend, but so recently ex that the friendship would be wasted right now. She thought she saw a flash, over heads and shoulders, of butter and sugar hair, and it made her stomach wobble. She walked over to the window, where she hoped that some summer might be seeping in. But no warmth could escape the street. The windows were so thick and firm that the sky beyond them looked stormy and faraway. The smooth steel frames showed no clasps or hinges. They would never give, or admit any of the elements. This cold came from somewhere else, and got her anyway.

A man approached her. He wore a linen suit with the sleeves and cuffs rolled up and no shoes or socks. He was very tall and had blown-back hair, like a man on television. He looked happy and confident and toasty. He smiled. She smiled back, and he swept his big hand toward the window.

"How'd you like to have a view like that?"

The girl peered at his suntanned face. "I wouldn't. The waterfront looks like the end of the earth in winter, all frozen over."

The man's mouth seemed to pause in a perfect crescent before becoming real again. "Just so, just so." He wasn't looking at her any more and sounded as though he were speaking to himself, so she made a move to walk away. Then, "Are you all right? You look . . . your fingernails are blue." He pointed at the hand holding the glass.

She could feel herself getting frozen to the spot, iced over, unable to move. She sighed in a gust. "I'm cold. I didn't know we'd have to take off our shoes." Her voice sounded like the wail of the wind. She hated that. They both looked down. Her toenails were blue, too.

His voice sounded like he was inquiring about pizza toppings over the phone. "Do you want to wear my socks?"

Her gaze snapped up from the floor to his wide mouth.

"I stuck them in my briefcase. I didn't fancy going sock-footed. Wanted to be *Miami Vice*, y'know? They won't match your dress, but you're welcome, if you like. . . ."

She'd forgotten about her warm-coloured dress, was too cold to care about clashing, anyway. She was trapped in an igloo-condo. Her boss would ask her about it on Monday if she left early. Another sip of her rye and ginger would solidify in her throat and she'd never speak again. The condo windows were sealed against the summer outside like the Arctic part of the biodome. She followed the man to the front hall. He rummaged through a pile of shoelaces and purse straps and found an old bulky brown satchel. He pulled out the socks singly, crumpled.

The socks were an electric ice, a brilliant pale blue that she'd never seen before. It was a new colour. Laid flat in her palm, they felt thick and cottony, not at all damp despite having been worn all day. She wondered if they would smell the way he looked, like a golf green in the sun, like thawed lake water. . . . The man was staring at her and she realized that her face was too close to the socks, far too close to sniffing them. She felt warm colour creep into her cheeks, which was nice but she was still embarrassed as she bent down. With her head close to her smoothly shaven shins, she was able to inhale deeply but all she smelled was the baked smell of cotton, the lemon of floor polish. As she straightened, she said, "These are great socks. They are a wonderful colour."

"Thanks. I love that blue. I have a coat that shade, too. I mean –" he pressed his lips tightly for a moment "– in winter, my winter coat matches them." In the pause, he gazed at her enveloped calves and the music went silent. "They look great on you." Then, on the big German stereo in the living room, a nasal whine filtered out. "It's Elvis Costello, it's 'American Without Tears,'" he told her.

She listened and nodded. A whole minute passed before she said, "It's in waltz time. That's not so common any more."

His lips pulled back from his teeth and his hands spread wide. "Well, then we shouldn't waste it." One arm shot straight out; the other hooked in front of him, reaching for her waist.

She stepped into his linen arms. When he whirled her into the living room the wind caught her hair again and her yellow skirt spun out around her knees and the smooth blue socks slid like blades on the polished wooden rink. The hostess passed by with a tray of flying-fish-roe canapés, looked up briefly, and altered her course so she wouldn't interrupt the dancers. Her friends widened their eyes and clutched their drinks. Maya leaned against a wall and thought about saunas.

The song ended. The man squeezed her hand and then pulled away. He had whirled her so fast that her pale skin was flushed and her heart was pulsing. She even felt a tiny drop of sweat trickle down under the collar of her sweater. She wanted to take the sweater off. She was not cold.

"I have to go," he said. He pointed toward the doorway, where three young men in suits with rolled sleeves and cuffs were standing slouched, looking impatient.

"I'll give you back your socks." She bent over and lifted up one foot.

He put a hand on her shoulder and stopped her. "It's okay. Keep them for the party, so you won't be cold."

"But how –"

"Now you'll have to find me, and I'll get to see you again." He left.

The girl had a good time at the party once she was warm. She ate canapés covered with tiny salty fish eggs and washed them down with rye and ginger, no ice. She talked and laughed, although not with Maya, who left early. And the girl asked everyone she talked to about a tall famous-looking man in an expensive suit. But no one knew who that man was, not even the hostess. It was very strange. Not even the hostess.

The party ended. She went home, tiptoed past her roommate, who was watching a cartoon about amoebas, and went to bed. In the morning the girl got up and did her laundry. She put the wintry socks in the delicate cycle and dried them with a pine fabric softener. Then she rolled them into a tight ball and put the ball in the corner of her handbag.

———

Summer was too short. The leaves got crunchy and the wind learned to bite. The fashion that year was for cashmere, which was petal-soft on delicate skin but let the chill run right through. The girl bought balls of 100% wool and knitted herself a thick toque and scarf. She tried to knit mittens but got stuck on the thumbs, so she wore two cashmere pairs instead.

The wind blew chunks of ice into her skin. Her eyes streamed with salt water and sadness. There were Christmas

lights in the window of the Indian restaurant that was supposed to be the best in the city. She opened the steamy glass
door eagerly, looking forward to the meal, the peppers, the
vinegar, cayenne, and cinnamon. She loved vindaloo. She
loved foods that made her sweat.

The waiter motioned her toward a coat rack where she
could hang her fisherman's jacket, her fuzzy cardigan, her
crooked scarf and tipsy hat. She stuffed everything into the
sleeve of her coat and put it on a wooden hanger that looked
strong enough to support it all. On the rack next to her coat
was another coat. This coat was the colour of the harbour in
a midday storm, or a January moon, or the heart of a flame. A
coat the colour of the socks in her bag.

When she took them out, the socks seemed a bit dingy
from being pressed against grocery receipts and pencils and
dirty change for the past few months. She felt guilty about
that. The warm round ball nestled in her cupped hands like a
chick or a candle. She could already feel the winter mist creeping under the doors and through the window panes; it moved
through her shirt and touched her skin. The restaurant was
crowded with the breath of many people, though, and a
peppery vapour burned in her nostrils. She slipped the roll of
blue, blue socks into the pocket of the blue, blue coat. As she
turned away from the coat rack, a flicker of too-long hair
blown by the wind caught her eye from the doorway. The
waiter pointed her toward a table in the far corner, blocked
from the draft of the door by a screen, near the heating regis-
ter. The girl was about to walk toward it, but then the Hindi
love song on the stereo changed to something else, a
Christmas song. It was "Fairytale of New York" by the Pogues.

It was in waltz time. The girl turned away from the warm spot. She went to the only other empty table, which was beside the icy window, but in view of the door, the coat-rack, and the fiery open kitchen. She sat down and waited to see what would happen next.

PATRICIA ROBERTSON

MY HUNGARIAN SISTER

first saw her looking out at me from a newspaper photograph: a small girl in a polka-dot headscarf, holding a rumpled doll. She stood, the smallest, among a group of children standing in a railway station; Euston, the caption said. They were refugees, a word I did not know, from Hungary, a country somewhere in dimmest Europe. In Europe, people did not speak English but wore peculiar costumes and were forever dancing on cobbled streets. My parents, who had spent their honeymoon in Paris, had spoken of *café crèmes* and the Arc de Triomphe, of walks along the Seine and *moules marinières*. My father, ludicrously, still wore the wool beret he'd brought back, as though our Lancashire street was a part of the continent.

Below the headline – "First Refugee Children Find Warm Welcome in Britain" – a story, datelined Vienna, spoke bafflingly of Soviet repression, of United Nations resolutions, of appeals by the Undersecretary for Foreign Affairs. I skipped to the end. The Hungarian refugees were arriving in Austria with nothing. One family had escaped on motorcycles, another in a hay wagon. An entire circus with three dancing bears, twenty dogs, and seven horses had arrived the previous evening. As for the children, many had been sent across the border with cards round their necks. *Please look after our young ones. We stay to fight to the last.*

I looked again at the girl in the photograph. Her eyes were large, dark, smudged with exhaustion. In her headscarf and pinafore dress, clutching the doll, she seemed burdened with some secret and unspeakable knowledge. What was it like to be sent, alone, to a place where you knew no one? Had her parents told her to be brave? Had she known, when she crossed the border, that she might never see them again?

I, however, could see her destiny. She would live right here in Wyecombe, she would sit at our table and share my bed. No longer some nameless child with a tag round her neck like a piece of luggage, she would be the confidante I'd always wanted, the perfect corrective to my lopsided, boy-heavy family. We – my family and I – would do what her parents had asked.

On some of the cards, so the newspaper said, the parents had written the word *szabadság*: freedom. That was what I would call her. Szaba, for short.

My father was then an assistant editor for our local newspaper, the *Lancastrian*. He often brought home the *Times* and the *Manchester Guardian* (for the view from the balcony and the view from the shop floor, he said) and quoted from them over the tea table, to my mother's annoyance. Soviet tanks had entered Budapest; troops with red stars on their shoulders were stationed at every street corner. And the government believes the Russians'll negotiate, he said. Can you imagine? It's obvious that poor Imre Nagy is going to be executed.

They wouldn't dare, my mother said, handing round the potted meat. Hadn't the Prime Minister sent a stiffly worded note? And did he have to discuss such things in front of the children?

The British Ambassador, actually, my father said. He had opened the *Guardian* again; my mother, defenceless, noisily stirred her tea. Our voice will not go out in vain to the gallant Hungarian people, my father quoted. Fine empty words that'll have no effect at all. If your church was doing its job, they'd be condemning the Russians from the pulpit.

My father came from a family of Northumbrian coal miners, my mother from Anglican clergy who invariably voted Tory. My grandfather had still not quite forgiven her for marrying a threat to the social order. On my last birthday, perhaps to provide protection against possible contamination, he had presented me with a Bible, my name embossed in gilt on its brown leather. He had also recently taken me out to tea at the Poplars, a restaurant favoured by what my father called the aspiring gentry. I was his only granddaughter, a reader and a scholar; people said I took after him. But how could I sit there eating cream buns among acres of white linen when in Hungary children were starving? There was no food in the shops and even twelve-year-olds had been given rifles.

Does she have to learn about the brutality of the world quite so early? my mother said that evening, when they thought I was asleep.

We can't keep it from her forever. Besides, death's a fact of life.

Farm deaths, my mother said. Cats or pigs. Not bloody uprisings.

What about the miners in Ledburgh, in 1920? Didn't *those* children watch their parents being shot? By British troops, no less?

Not by *my* ancestors, my mother said stiffly.

They certainly didn't stop it. They probably prayed for victory. Believed God was on their side.

At the moment, God was, for some inexplicable reason, on the side of the Russians. Not for the first time, despite our weekly attendance at church, I agreed with my father, who had explained that it all had to do with another religion called Communism, whose high priest was Stalin. Blasphemy, my mother said. My father, laughing, said he was an old apostate and could say anything he liked.

My family had done a singularly poor job of producing females. My father was an only child; my mother, like me, had two brothers, a bachelor country curate and a bank manager who had sired only sons. I was followed by Timothy, aged four, and Matthew, nine months, who I'd been certain would be a girl. I had prayed every night for a sister, but God hadn't listened. Too distracted, perhaps, by African hunger and the Suez crisis, though the denial of what was surely a simple request was further evidence for my father's theories.

Szaba was the perfect solution, the only way to fill that four-year gap between me and Tim. She would also be our own personal support for the Hungarian nation. At my school, a fund for the refugees was being established. We might give part of our allowances, or bring items for a bake sale. My mother's cakes were a disaster – lumpen for the proletariat, my father had joked, though only once – so I gave threepence, half my weekly allotment, and bravely went without my dolly mixture, my licorice allsorts. We helped pack food hampers, including oranges from Spain; apparently Hungarian children had never tasted them. The school would send them to a refugee reception centre in London.

The other half of my allowance (no more weekly comics) I put into a jar marked "Szaba." At night I took out the photo I'd clipped from the paper. You're going to have a home very soon, I told her. Once or twice I swear I saw her look back at me with those large exhausted eyes, saw the corners of her mouth lift in the tiniest smile. I would show her my doll collection, my diary, my secret hiding places. I would teach her two-ball and hop-scotch and double dutch. I would ask if her parents, too, had arguments, if her father ever walked out of the house in the middle of one. At night, in the dark, we would hold each other, and not even the creaking staircase would make us afraid.

We are standing at the station. The train slows, the door opens, and there she is, holding her doll and smiling shyly. I step forward. Hello, Szaba, I say. Welcome to Wyecombe. I say it in her language, from a piece of paper written out by my Polish piano teacher, whose husband is Hungarian. Now there is a real smile. My parents also step forward and embrace her. Even Timothy says hello. I take her hand and we walk together, already a family, out to the waiting car.

We sit side by side in the back and I point out the school, the library, the street my grandfather lives on. Does she have a grandfather, back in Hungary? But perhaps it is best not to ask this. She takes off her headscarf, revealing thick dark curly hair, the kind I've always wanted. When we get home I will brush it and let her borrow my hair ribbons.

In Budapest the first frosts had arrived; two square miles in the centre of the city lay in ruins. Szaba, if she knew, would be sick with worry; she might be having nightmares. I decided instead that she was from a small town in the south where there were fewer Russian troops. Her parents were hiding in the forest with the other partisans, leaving at night to plant grenades and stock up with food. They were dirty, in rags, but undaunted, and they knew God had secretly changed sides. Unfortunately, brave as they were, I would have to kill them off – otherwise we would not be able to adopt Szaba – but we would find out, after all this was over, that they had died fighting. .

I had read about a thirteen-year-old boy who set fire to the Russian tanks and then shot the crews as they came out. He was Szaba's older brother, of course. The new Hungarian government would award him a posthumous medal, which they would send to Szaba. She would keep it in a special box and take it out on his birthday.

I told no one else about Szaba. I did, however, ask my father about the refugee children and what happened to them. He said they were sent to hostels and then on to relatives or friends, if they had any. Some, he thought, would end up in foster homes. Perhaps their parents would be able to escape, and then they'd be reunited.

Hang on, Szaba! Help is coming!

It was my mother I approached first. Her Ladies' Aid group was knitting scarves for the refugees, and I asked if I might make one too. How thoughtful, she said, and showed me how to cast on, how to knit and purl. I chose the colours of the Hungarian flag, red and green and white. I saw Szaba in the scarf, walking down the street with me, hand in hand. At school I would explain that her parents were freedom fighters and her older brother was a soldier. That would impress the boys. At recess they'd crowd round and ask if she had any bullets as souvenirs.

Our church was helping to sponsor two families, my mother said; they were going to settle in our area. Perhaps we too could sponsor a refugee, I said. Perhaps there was a child who needed a place to stay. My mother looked at me sharply. We've no room, she said; we need a larger house as it is. It's not right for you to keep sharing a bedroom with Timothy.

But if it's a girl, she could sleep with me, I said.

That's very selfless, Catherine. But I've my hands full with the three of you. The answer's no.

My father said that if it was up to him he'd take in a houseful of bairns, but the final word was my mother's. I asked my piano teacher if Szaba could live with them instead. They had no children, after all, and her husband spoke Hungarian. But she was too old, she said, and her husband wasn't well. Who was this Szaba, and how did I know her?

I hadn't meant to reveal her name. I'd heard about her at school, I said. Her name had been on one of the hampers we'd sent to London. Mrs. Berényi paused. She too had received such a hamper in a refugee camp in Switzerland after the war. She had lost everything then – her first husband to invading German troops, her mother to pneumonia, her baby to starvation after her milk dried up. A younger cousin, a teenager, had fought with the Polish resistance, but had been caught and shot.

I hadn't known that such things happened to people I knew. I thought of this cousin, and Mrs. Berényi's baby, and Szaba's brother, lined up in a row on the ground, eyes closed. What brutes the Russians and Germans were. Why couldn't people live together in peace? If the Russians ever invaded England, Szaba and I would throw stones at the soldiers as they marched down our street, and then we would hide in the unused mill behind the school where no one could find us.

No, my mother said. I've told you, Catherine. Absolutely not. And you're not to keep pestering me. She had found me with the photograph of Szaba when I was supposed to be doing my homework, and threatened to tear it up. All right, I won't, on condition that you forget the whole idea. We are not, and I repeat *not*, adopting her or anyone else. Is that clear?

At night, as we lie in bed together, Szaba tells me her story. When the Russians invaded, her parents decided to send her out of the country before the borders were sealed. Her brother István too, but he wouldn't go. That night – a dark night, the moon obscured by clouds – they slipped out of the house and across farmers' fields, heading west. They walked through forest and across bog. They had

*to ford a river. Szaba's shoes filled with mud. When she couldn't
walk any further her father carried her on his shoulders. They came
to a row of trees with the lights of Austria on the other side. She
was to walk to the nearest house and knock on the door.*

It won't be long, Szaba. We won't be separated long.

Anya. Apa. Szabadág. *Already she was forgetting what they
meant.*

It was Mrs. Berényi who suggested I write to the Red Cross. I
had come for my regular Thursday piano lesson, two weeks
before the Christmas holidays. Outside, frost lay on the hedges
and bare branches pricked a cotton-wool sky. In Hungary,
where many people in the cities were without heat, it was even
colder. My father said the Russians were deporting able-bodied
Hungarians to Russia for slave labour. Past bombed-out build-
ings and across snowy steppes the trains moved, slow, burdened,
unremarked, until they disappeared below the horizon.

After the lesson Mrs. Berényi set a glass of sugared tea and
one of her Christmas *beigli* before me. So. We are still thinking of the refugees. Such a credit to your parents, Catherine.

I'm worried about Szaba, Mrs. Berényi. She needs a home.

The Red Cross will be looking after her. Mrs. Berényi
cradled her glass of tea in her thin hands. They helped László
and I, after the war, when we were in that camp in Switzerland.

But if she came, this Szaba, in her polka-dot headscarf.
Faced with an actual child, my parents wouldn't be able to
turn her away.

Why, Mrs. Berényi asked, was I interested in this particular
one?

I could not say that our destinies were intertwined, that she had been sent here for a reason. Instead I showed her the photograph.

Maybe her family knows your husband. Maybe they're even relatives.

Most of her husband's family, Mrs. Berényi said, had been shot, or deported, or had disappeared. But perhaps, through the Red Cross, we could find out what had happened to her.

I waited, daily, for a reply. I slipped round to the Berényis' every day after tea until my mother demanded an explanation. The letter arrived just before Christmas. Mrs. Berényi read it out loud when I arrived for my last piano lesson of the year.

> Dear Mrs. Berényi,
> Thank you for your interest in the plight of the Hungarian refugees. We have been unable to determine which child you referred to, but we can assure you that she is being well taken care of. We hope that in time many of the children will be reunited with their parents. Thank you also for your kind donation.

But Szaba would not be reunited with her parents. Hadn't I killed them off? I showed my father the letter. Mrs. Berényi was trying to find a child whose family had been friends of her husband's, I said. My father offered to write a story for his paper. It ran on page 22, next to the Out and About column: "Girl in Headscarf Sought by Local Couple." Mrs. Berényi was quoted as saying that she and her husband had wanted to contribute to the child's first Christmas away from home.

I waited, again, for another letter, this time from the family who had taken Szaba in, or Szaba herself. Of course she would not be able to write in English, but Mr. Berényi could translate. At night I took out the photograph and stared at it with furious intensity. Listen, Szaba, wherever you are. I'm here in Wyecombe, waiting for you. Just for you.

Christmas lacked a certain sparkle, though my parents took us to the pantomime in Manchester. On my first day back at school after the holidays, three shabbily dressed children stood beside the headmistress at general assembly. They were introduced to us as Ferenc, Emil, and Márta. I had summoned not one Hungarian refugee, but three! The youngest, Márta, was assigned to the year below mine. She was thin and plain, and she wore no headscarf, but it would be churlish to accuse God of ignoring my requests.

At recess, I asked her to join me. She had stained brown teeth and a habit of pulling at the threads of her jumper. She had been taken in, she explained in broken English, by a Romanian family who lived nearby. I showed her how to play hopscotch, but she wanted only to watch. DP lover, said one of the boys, brushing my shoulder. I took Márta by the hand and walked to another part of the schoolyard, where we chewed toffee together in silence until recess was over.

I was allowed to invite Márta home for tea. She wore a strange frilled blouse and a skirt two sizes too big. She did not know how to use a fork and drank her tea out of the saucer. Upstairs I showed her my new velvet dress, the games I had been given for Christmas, but she sat on the bed with her hands folded and shook her head when I suggested we play with my dolls.

I brought out the photo of Szaba, thinking perhaps Márta knew her, but she burst into tears and began saying something over and over in Hungarian. My mother came running upstairs. What on earth was the matter? She put her arm round Márta and glared at me.

I didn't do a thing, Mum. I just showed her that photo.

Of all the – Didn't you stop to think it might bring back memories? That she probably saw herself in that train station?

No. I hadn't. I'd wanted to show that I knew her story. Here was Szaba, with a different face and a different name. I knew her parents were freedom fighters and her brother was a hero who had killed Russian soldiers. *Szabadág*, I said after my mother had left. *Szabadág*, and I pointed to the photograph. But Márta pointed to herself. *Halott*, she said. Dead. And then she lay down on the bed and closed her eyes.

I did not invite her again. In the playground I avoided her; I told my classmates that I could not understand her, which was partially true. Somewhere, no doubt, she had parents, and after a while they would find each other. Meanwhile she was with her Romanian family, who were also from that murky continent. She must feel more comfortable there than with us.

But what of Szaba? There had been some mistake, after all, in the fact that Márta had been sent instead. Szaba's photo had appeared in the *Guardian*; it was to them I would turn. I found the address just below the masthead and wrote a careful letter. A journalist from the paper called my parents. A heartwarming story, he said, about hands across frontiers and all that. My father said I had the makings of a politician, my mother that I was trying to shame her in front of everybody. I was merely practising Christian compassion, my father said. My mother said she didn't need her religion thrown in her face, thank you very much, and even Jesus had had his limits.

A few days later the journalist rang back. He'd made some inquiries of his own, he said, just to put my mind at rest. He'd managed to track the girl to Salisbury, where distant relatives had taken her in. They did not want any names released; they feared reprisals against those still in Hungary. They thanked the journalist, and my family, for our interest.

I folded the photograph of Szaba and put it at the bottom of my jewellery box. The girl with the polka-dot scarf would stand there forever, at Euston Station; I preferred not to think about what had become of her. At school, Márta had disappeared, sent, so someone said, to join her parents in Germany. I asked no questions. A few months later, when my mother mentioned her name, at first I didn't know who she was talking about.

Years later, I stood in the reception hall of a London embassy, where a woman was introduced to me. A colleague on another newspaper, my host said. Her name was Juliska. Her father had fled to Britain from Hungary after the war. To make conversation I asked whether she'd known any families who had taken in Hungarian refugees. Yes, she said, her own. A boy of thirteen named István. He was a professor now at some technical institute in Germany. He had written a book about his experiences. She could give me the title.

I thanked her and said I would read it. But I never did.

ALICE PETERSEN

AFTER SUMMER

Jake and I grew up without a mother, which wasn't that bad, although we ate a lot of boiled peas. Back when we were kids, before Maybelle came into the picture, Dad rented a boathouse every year for the whole of August, up on a lake near Shawinigan. He spent the summer months growing a fat Hemingway moustache while the sun darkened his shoulders to the colour of beer. We weren't supposed to sleep at the boathouse, but in early August, when the concrete city had baked hard in the sun, Dad would drive us up to the lake on Friday nights. We'd light citronella candles to keep the mosquitoes off, eat rubbery pizza, and drink warm juice out of the cooler. When the bats came out we'd go up into the woods to pee before going to sleep in a row on the boathouse floor, listening to the water lapping and Dad breathing in the dark.

On Saturday mornings, Dad sat in the boathouse attic typing up the poems that he carried in his head during the rest of the year. The poems were mainly about women once glimpsed through panes of frosted glass, because he was a mail carrier with two kids and that's about as close as he ever got. If you stood at the bottom of the ladder to the attic you could hear Dad up there groaning over lines about galoshes and garden paths, white terriers and white negligees, the day-long ning-nong of the bell and the endless wait for a snug fit in scented flesh.

While Dad worked at his poems, Jake and I squatted on the dock making fat duck farting noises by blowing through blades of grass. Sometimes we would stir the water with sticks, or catch horseflies and hand-deliver them into the webs of spiders. Dad was in his confessional and we were being mostly good. Eventually Dad would climb back down the ladder, his skin smelling of hot pine boards and the edgy stench of the bats that lived behind the rafters, and then we would all swing off the rope on the tree and drop into the water.

I have this vision of Dad at the lake during the long summers, emerging from the waves, his chest hair plastered into dripping points. Shaggy Dad, Poseidon Dad, ever-strong Dad, and Jake and I screaming and clinging to him like monkeys while he dunked us up and down. And eventually he would say, "Clear off, I feel a poem coming on," and he would grab a couple of beers out of the cooler dug into the shallows and disappear up the ladder into the attic to write, while we sidled off to the cliffs to look for fossils.

Once we didn't clear off. Instead we dragged a ladder out of the grass and propped it up against the boathouse wall. Jake was just peering into the window at the top when a rotten rung of the ladder gave way and he fell and knocked himself out.

"Dad's got no clothes on and he's crying," he said when he woke up, by which time Dad was fully dressed and driving us into town as fast as he could.

It hadn't occurred to us that Dad might be unhappy, because we weren't, and it was summertime, and Dad was just Dad. We knew he drank at night on the boathouse steps, but it didn't bother us. The more beer he drank, the more bottles there were to get a refund on.

Just after we turned fourteen, Dad started dating Maybelle, and that was the end of summers at the lake, because there was no plug at the boathouse for her hair dryer. Maybelle was a secretary at our high school. She took it on to rescue Dad from the two giant squid choking him in their tentacled embrace. First she moved in and began cooking balanced meals, which in itself wasn't a bad thing, but then she persuaded Dad to give up mail delivery and open a dry-cleaning business. There was an office out back of the store where Maybelle talked on the phone to tardy clients, threatening to send their suits and dresses to Colombia in a container ship if they did not come to collect them. "Most companies don't bother to phone," she would say. My father pressed the trousers. The heat made his hair damp and curled it behind his ears. I worked the cash after school. I liked the punking noise the receipts made when you stuck them on the spike. Jake refused to have anything to do with it.

A couple of years after Dad hooked up with Maybelle, Jake slipped the net and hitchhiked to Big Sur. Four years passed and Maybelle spotted him on a home-renovating show, making a plywood stereo cabinet on a suburban front lawn, satisfying women across North America with the kerthunk of his nail gun and the hiss and judder of the compressor. He was giving the camera his long, lazy grin and he had his ball cap at a howdy-pardner tilt. The dentist always said that Jake had too many teeth, but he had enough for television.

After Jake lit out I stayed on, typing out my angst one finger at a time on Dad's Olivetti in awful, badly spaced, rhyming verse about hideous misunderstandings and imagined perfect communion. After I had written each poem, I would shred it and let my geriatric gerbils make a nest of my thoughts. I was slightly chubby, hopelessly normal.

I haven't spent my life looking for a mother, and I certainly haven't looked for one in Maybelle. Maybelle keeps her hair pretty. She sews sofa cushions. She is a wreath-of-dried-flowers-with-seasonal-bear-on-the-front-door kind of person. I haven't missed mothering, but I'm kind of missing Dad. Maybelle has him cornered like a bull, down on his Hemingway knees, helpless beneath the weight of house and car payments. Every day he's slapped by the coats on the electric rack at the dry cleaner's as they flare out and twirl around the corner. But he seems happy. I have to be honest about that. Maybe Dad has a good time between Maybelle's satin sheets.

The other weekend I went out to buy a chair just like the one Dad used to sit on to write his poetry. Dad's chair had a woven seat made of some kind of hide, thick and yellow like old cooked pasta. We always thought of it as catgut since Dad emitted such excruciating yowls during his bouts of work. The chair had no screws in it – just wooden plugs, and when Dad stretched back, the chair creaked from the hip joint. Not a comfortable chair, but a speaking chair that moaned along with Dad's efforts to express himself. Of course we had to leave it behind in the boathouse with all the other stuff that was never ours.

I drove out across the plain toward Ste-Eulalie, thinking of the time when it had been boreal forest, and how the rustling leaves must have roared in the wind, like the sea in the fall. My dog had her head out the passenger window. Flecks of saliva whipped off her tongue and stuck to the rear door. There never was a dog with so much saliva, or such perpetual anticipation of the good to come.

At the antique store, a dog with a golden plume of a tail rushed out to sniff at my dog and my shoes. The store was a real barn of a place, hung with moose heads and ancient egg beaters and leather pouches of oxidizing fishing hooks. Most of the furniture had been scraped and repainted, as if the years had not given it enough story, so story had to be added to it.

I asked about chairs and was directed upstairs to a stifling room under the rafters, filled with golden light that came through panels let into the ceiling. At one end were stacks of tables – end tables, side tables with barley-twist legs, dining-room tables, bedside tables with drawers, washstands – so many surfaces for putting down cups, saucers, books, type-writers, and beer bottles. And hundreds of chairs spooning into each other, battered, scraped, loose-bottomed, straw-filled, hidebound chairs, which meant that there were hundreds of lapsed poets, hundreds of adult children looking for lost fathers, and hundreds of family stories about step-mothers – which, when you came down to it, weren't so different one from another. The weight of all those chairs hanging among the rafters filled me with panic.

After Maybelle came, there was none of the tangy essence of bat left about my father. The moist air of dry cleaning softened Dad's poems and turned them to powdery mould. And now he's going to marry Maybelle, and after I've signed him over as a going concern I wonder when I'll be talking to him again, because it's his life now, and he's chosen to live like that, with her and her dried flowers. I just wish that Jake would slouch on in with his arms crossed over his chest and smile in his lazy summer-dog way, because I really want to take him out for a beer and ask him if he thinks that we somehow made Dad feel smothered when we clung on to him. I mean, when he dunked us in the water, did he ever wish that he could let us go? And now that we are twenty, has he at last let us go? And if he has, what is it like to tread water alone, without even a chair to hold onto when the spring floods come?

NICOLE DIXON

HIGH-WATER MARK

My sister thinks I gave my mom cancer. Lauren's become an expert on death since her baby died.

I heard *hemorrhoid* when my mom said *thyroid*. I was almost laughing except Lauren started crying, so I realized it wasn't hemorrhoids, even though she cries at everything now. I decided I wasn't gonna sit on that couch with my sister and watch my mom's eyebrows and eyelashes spill out of her face. My mom saw me looking at Lauren and then her and back at Lauren, and she said, You have something to say, Ainslee?

"I'm going to Robbie's." And I went to my room, grabbed some shit, and left.

I have a summer job in the gift shop up at the Cape. The Cape's a big cliff way up high and way out in the water and way far away from town. I had to buy a truck – a blue and white Ford – to get myself up there and back, but Robbie drives it mostly since he's twenty-five and has a licence and I can't get my beginners yet. *Had* a licence, I should say.

The gift shop looks like a lighthouse and it's the first thing the tourists see when they park their big, shiny, American vans and all their kids pile out like clowns and squeeze into the shop. They ask if this is the lighthouse they've driven all this way to see and I say, no, the real one's down that hill and they unfold the folded T-shirts with their ice cream fingers and shuffle the postcards and stink up the bathroom and grumble about the drive up the road, like it's personally *my* responsibility to pave it, even though it's the first time they've *really* used their SUVs. And then they complain about having to walk down the hill and ask, could they drive? and ask, could I take their picture? and ask, how much are the T-shirts? and ask, do I see many whales? and ask, what do I do around here for fun?

Tourism's a verbal assembly line.

No you can't drive, you should walk, Fatso, and I'll tell you the price of T-shirts if you're actually gonna buy one. And for fun? I smoke and drive fast and drink beer and get stoned and fuck Robbie.

"I hike the beach and watch for whales and pick wild-flowers."

"Wish I lived your life," they sigh.

Sometimes when Robbie remembers to pick me up, we do hike down to the beach and drink beer he's brought and watch the rip tide rip at the rocks. The waves crash higher than our heads and we're soon soaked and freezing but screaming and smashing our bottles into the wind. The rocks are flat and curved like worn stairs, and once Robbie pulled me into a kinda cave and lifted me up onto a ledge. I wrapped my legs around him as he yanked down my jeans and we never noticed the tide coming in until we were done and Robbie's feet were soaked. We had to slip and slide back up the rocks. We sat for a bit while the tide swallowed our little love nest. My dad drowned in those rips, and that's how quick it must have happened – a blink of breath then lobster bait.

At night, driving off the Cape, there's this one curve where you can see the lights of the village, and just right there, Refugee Cove looks like a glittery city, all lit up for a party. Then down we go to the main road, to Robbie's, pulling into his driveway. At that moment, it's the most his house looks like a trailer, which is exactly what it is.

Lauren calls me Robbie's little woman but living with him feels like one long sleepover. Pajama drama, pillowfighting.

Lauren's over, trying to be my mom 'cause Mom won't be my mom and Lauren wants so bad to be a mom.

"Why don't you come home?"

"I am home."

"You're getting stupider. Sunbathing naked on that boat? With all those guys?"

"Robbie was there. It wasn't all day, and I was just topless. *They* were topless. Some of those guys have bigger tits than me."

"This is what's making her sick."

I look where Lauren's looking, at my feet on the coffee table, beside my math textbook, some rolling papers, pot crumbs. Robbie's smells like the last slurps of week-old beer in the bottom of a bottle, and there's plenty of that around.

"Robbie got me to quit smoking."

"Smoking's better for you than Robbie."

"I'm not making her sick."

"You're not helping."

"You get cancer, you get cancer. What I'm doing has nothing to do with it."

"I think you're wrong. If you're happy and a good person, good stuff happens. You surround yourself with crap, crap happens. Her being happy could get her better."

"Is that what you believe? That being happy and good will get you a new life? Then how come Dad's dead? I don't mean people who are good have bad things happen. I mean, people who are good maybe aren't so good."

The world doesn't need any more people, so it picks at them like scabs and off they go. Yeah, Refugee Cove could stand a few more kids so the school doesn't shut down. I could barely tell Lauren was pregnant at her graduation – she just looked fat under her gown. If they need kids though, there's plenty. Spend some time with me at the gift shop. The way parents yell at or ignore their kids? Tourists are like blackflies.

No one knew Lauren's kid's heart was fucked until she was born. I was an aunt for six days. I liked being Aunt Ainslee; I had plans to make those the kid's first words.

After her kid died, Lauren packed all her baby stuff into a box and left it at the end of her driveway. I poked around at all the toys and bottles and books and clothes while I was waiting for the bus, which started coming just when I found the teeny yellow toque she wore in the hospital, so I grabbed it and shoved it in my jacket pocket and hopped on the bus. All morning I kept thinking about all that little little stuff that'd had such big big plans so I skipped school at lunch but by the time I got home the box was gone.

When I moved into Robbie's I took that toque with me. Sometimes when Robbie's sleeping I put it on my left hand like a mitt. It covers my three middle fingers, not even halfway.

The one time I held my niece, her head rested right there in those three fingers. Lauren still hadn't given her a name, and never did, but when the baby opened her eyes, it was like she was asking for one.

Robbie smoked me up before work today. I can't tell if time's moving faster or slower or if the T-shirts are cold or wet.

Vince is my boss and he's sixty-seven but looks younger than most dads and lives in the woods where he grows blueberries and weed. What's a bigger deal than growing weed, since tonnes of people I know grow weed, is that he moved here from Alberta, when most people from here talk about moving to Alberta.

My sister had this job till she got pregnant. I think Vince likes us working here 'cause he fucked my mom years ago. I'm not so sure on that, but Lauren would roll her eyes and make gagging sounds whenever he came around. Lauren remembers Dad more than me, so it's more a deal for her.

Vince comes to drop off peanuts and coffee filters and asks, Sell anything today, Ainslee? I can't stop staring at his dirty fingernails. Is he cooking lunch with those?

"I woulda sold a T-shirt if we had greys in extra-large."

"Two years ago, large was fine. Now it's extra."

"Busy at the restaurant?"

"Almost outta chowder. Cloudy days aren't BLT days."

Talk so small you can't see it.

An old guy stumbles in, knee socks and sandals, Tilley hat, Peggy's Cove sweatshirt, large. Especially 'cause Vince is there, I put on my big Cape smile that says, *Welcome, Tourist. Yes, we have T-shirts in your size.*

"Can I help you?"

"Oh, ooh. Ha. Where are your restrooms?"

I point to the door beside him.

Good thing Vince raises his voice.

"The bike tour guys are coming later. Can you stay an extra hour to help them bring down their luggage? Cyclone Tours. They've been here before."

"Cyclops Tours."

"Hey, Ainslee – no more work weed."

Sometimes, I get the nervous butterflies, like one day at low tide, Robbie took me out in the truck and we spun doughnuts around in the harbour, red, rotten mud spraying in through the window and all over our faces. It made me laugh like crazy, but I got butterflies too. Not just in my stomach – on the tops of my hands and all around my thighs and in the middle of my throat. It's how my mom must feel. Her thyroid's this nervous butterfly in her throat. She wants to swallow it down but it's fucked up her swallowing so it's gotta become a part of her breathing until it gets too big and she can't even breathe anymore.

Tourists are like that – cancer cells. They don't belong and they fuck up the places they visit.

I never want to be a tourist, never want to just watch the rip tides but learn how to swim with them.

The Cyclops catches up with me. Cyclone Tours are regular, three-season customers so we've shot the shit before. I think he's plucked his monobrow.

"Looking forward to September?" he asks.

"First it's tourists, then hurricanes."

Robbie has my truck and he's late, so we're footing brick luggage down to the guesthouse instead of four-wheel driving. These cyclists freaking *biked* here, they've got the muscles, but it's the gift shop girl who's bricklaying.

"I always meant to ask what happened to the girl who worked here last summer."

"She's my sister and she had a baby."

Cyclops hits a loose rock and nearly drops the luggage.

"She had a baby?"

"Yeah, but it died."

Then he does fall, him and the luggage down flat. Nothing cracks open, no blood. My hands are too full to help him but I pause and watch. He's backstroking through his dust, then he twists around like a beetle and he's got the luggage and he's suddenly ahead of me.

"She still in town?" he yells. He's marching his cyclist calves.

"You know her and her boyfriend's house? Two over from . . . my mom's?"

"Yep, yep."

We reach the end of the path. It opens like the jaw of a beast, all waves and sky and rowdy wind. Over the Valley, black clouds are choking the sun.

"I'm stunned." Cyclops eyes the edge.

Vince calls them Repeats. The year-five honeymooners. The groupies. We like them, not only 'cause they bring us gifts, offerings for the view, but because they know you can't keep this landscape in a frame. They come back for the high, the shock. Each trip, they need to touch the fire to remember it's hot.

But there are the others, the ones who'll see those storm clouds and blame us for the rain and the roads it'll soon turn to gullies. So I'm glad when I see Robbie driving down in my truck, though too fast for the rutted road, aiming straight for us.

"How come you're pissed and won't let me drive?"

"Why were you talking to Bike Boy?"

"I meant drunk pissed. Lauren and I call him Cyclops."

The rain is crazy-loud on the roof of the truck so it sounds like we're fighting before we are.

"Lauren fucked the monster," he says.

We're driving underwater.

"Fuck off, no way."

"He was hitch-hiking to the Cape sometime last October not too far from your mom's, so I give him a ride. Says, 'You know Lauren McPhee?' 'Yeah, she's my buddy's girlfriend. Going to meet him now at his camp. Why?' I ask. All he says is he didn't know she had a boyfriend. Says nothing the rest of the way, I drop him off at the gift shop and he says it again. Then he gets out, says, 'Sorry,' holds his hands up like, 'don't shoot,' closes the door. Don't see him again till now."

"Last October . . ." I think. "Was around when we found out about Mom." My thighs are fluttering. "But so what? It wasn't me, it wasn't you, it's between Lauren and Mike."

"And their kid if it *was* Mike's."

"She's dead and you're driving too fast."

"Slut could run in the family."

"Fuck off, Robbie. Robbie!"

The truck's sliding instead of driving. It's the last hill before Refugee Cove except I can't see Refugee Cove, just the edge of the Cape then nothing, nothing's out my window, the front tire's going over except there's a tree and we stop. I am a quivering insect.

"Ainslee?"

Gravity's outside my door. I crawl over Robbie, straddle him. He leans to my neck, lips puckering to kiss or puke, but I lean further and open his door, jump out, start walking home. Not the trailer. Home home.

Lauren's there, instead of Mom.

"She went in a helicopter."

I am made of rain. I go to my room to change.

Lauren and I pass the trailer on our way to Halifax the next morning. My truck's in the yard, front end like a punched nose.

By Truro I almost ask Lauren about Cyclops. Then I don't. My niece is dead and soon Mom will be too.

"When it happens," Lauren's saying, her voice post-storm calm, "her ashes –"

"Off the Cape. Her and Dad . . ." Little Sister's crying.

"Will you do it with me?"

On-coming traffic is steady. Camper vans are stuffed with deflated beach balls, lawn chairs, coolers, families. Licence plates of every colour. It's late August.

From my back pocket I get the yellow toque, pull it over my three fingers and hold it up for Lauren to see. Her eyes widen. She takes one hand off the steering wheel and grabs my fingers, bringing them and the toque to her nose, her cheek, her neck, her stomach. Doesn't let go.

GRANT BUDAY

THE CURVE OF THE EARTH

Jay's mother was six-feet-one so spotting her was easy, even though a life-long habit of stooping to hide her height had curved her spine and rounded her shoulders. Even from the middle of the Piazza San Marco he could tell something was wrong. Had they been seasick? Robbed? Or had she merely grown old? Resentment replaced his anticipation at the prospect of seeing his parents, and then guilt overrode it.

Shorter, his father was harder to spot. It still bugged Jay that he hadn't inherited his mother's height. He didn't need to be six-feet-one, though five-eleven would've been nice, even five-ten. But five-seven? His mother often walked with her hand on her husband's arm. If she had been a tree – bent, ornamental, bearing some small tart fruit – she'd have had to be propped up with a post.

Jay called out a self-conscious, "Mom!" and then, trying not to flinch, he prepared himself to be kissed, yet she didn't kiss him, she draped herself over him and wept. Frightened, embarrassed, he tried seeing past her shoulder. "Where's Dad?"

"Constanta."

"Romania?"

"They say he owes back taxes. Forty-six years."

"*Taxes?*"

She nodded again and wiped her tears on a napkin stamped with the cruise line logo, a gold ship on a blue sea.

He'd intended to take his parents to Caffé Florian for lunch. Now, reeling, he decided to go straight to the hotel, but that meant a crowded *vaporetto* and a walk, or a gondola, which meant legalized extortion. Twenty years in Venice and he'd never yet paid for a gondola, a chronic cheapness inherited from his father. They needed a drink. He picked up both suitcases and led her across the piazza into the Calle Flubera to Giacomo's and ordered her a double gin and tonic.

"But he's got a Canadian passport!"

"They say he's still a Romanian citizen."

Jay found that eerie. He was fourteen before learning his father had changed his name from Pavel Bogza to Paul Bond. He'd been fascinated and a little appalled at the time, and would repeat to himself, *Jay Bogza*, and shudder at the alien sound. Bogza. He'd imagined some small, dark goblin of a man.

"Forty-six years of back taxes," said Jay, awed at the very thought of what that would amount to. His father had spent his life reusing teabags and keeping the heat at sixty-four all through winter despite the fact that he made an excellent salary as a university librarian. Better the old man had slipped and broken his hip. "Did you talk to him?"

"They just took him out of the disembarkation line. He said stay aboard, get a lawyer. The ship's officials agreed. I said no, but there were police, soldiers. Oh God . . ." she said, as if only now realizing the full horror of what she'd done.

Jay gripped her thin wrist, which felt disturbingly like cutlery rolled in a damp napkin.

———

"I look forward to meeting her," Lena had said last night. "We will talk and I learn many thing."

Jay doubted his mother would exchange confidences with Lena. She and his mother were the same age, sixty; in five days Jay would turn forty. Statistically speaking that meant he was over halfway through his life, a thought so crippling that it could stop him in the street and reduce him to a sick sweat. Canadian males averaged seventy-eight point two years of age; Italian males seventy-five point two. He'd now lived as many years in Italy as in his native Canada. Had he lost three years because of this? If he left now, could he regain them? As for what his father would think of Lena, well, he never knew what he thought. Maybe he and Lena would reminisce about Romania, but he doubted that too.

———

Having settled his mother in her hotel, Jay clumped up the stone steps to the apartment, once an attic in a lumber warehouse. It was stifling in the summer and smelled of hot rugs in the winter due to the electric heater. Two narrow windows, the only natural light, faced north over a *rio terra*, a filled-in canal.

He found Lena doing the standing splits, her forehead to the wall. "So?" she asked without moving, as if whispering to the brick. By the time he'd described everything, she'd swung her leg down and was shouting. "You left her in a hotel? Alone?" She raised her arm to slap him. She slapped him a lot.

In an hour he was back again, this time with his mother. Lena opened her arms in a massive embrace while Jay towed the suitcases to the spare room, a bed behind a Japanese screen, the little plastic wheels on the suitcases whirring quietly on the rugs then loudly on the planks. The apartment was one long, low room decorated with Turkish wall hangings and posters stolen from the annual Giotto exhibition in Padua, *The Scourging of Christ, Jesus Climbs to Calvary, The Crucifixion.* Philodendrons, the only plants that could survive the gloom, slumped in pots.

Lena and his mother were soon seated knee to knee on the couch, his mother nodding "Yes, yes," as Lena gripped both her hands and counselled her. The last of the daylight cast a medieval aura over the scene, as if his mother was confessing to the abbess of a nunnery.

Lena knew he was anxious about seeing his parents. Lying in bed last night, she'd watched him pace until she couldn't bear it. "Jay. Come." She'd held out one hand and he'd obeyed; she'd always be his master. After five years there was still an edge of illicitness about sex with Lena, like being taken to bed by a favourite aunt, something he liked but of late had begun to make him uneasy. Even when he initiated their love-making, she took control, directing him, turning him, getting on top, using him like a device.

Now she was counselling Jay's mother. "I have cousin," she said. "I make some call." She placed her forefinger upon his mother's frocked knee. "But I tell you something for fucking sure. You will have to pay."

His mother sagged.

Lena slumped in commiseration. Theatre. Typical. Jay wanted to tell her to fuck off. She wore an embroidered crimson top from Rajastan, sewn with bits of mirror. Her shoulder-length hair was straight and silver.

"What about the Canadian consul?" Jay asked.

"*Consul.*" The disdain in Lena's voice was as thick as her accent. She didn't deign to even look at him as she spoke. "If your father he like to spend a year in jail while the bureaucrat they play their game, okay maybe he don't pay. Pay *dollars*. But he will pay with time – time in Romanian jail. How old he is?"

"Sixty-six," said Jay's mother.

"No." The word slammed with the finality of a cell door. Lena was shaking her head again. "No. You don't want to know Romanian jail when you are sixty-six. In Romania most men are dead by sixty-six." This last fact seemed to give her grim satisfaction, as if Romanian men deserved it.

The light was now gone and the apartment chilly. Jay went around switching on the lamps in their shawl-draped shades then plugged in the heater nearest the women.

"But okay," Lena relented. "Tomorrow we talk to the consul in Roma. Maybe who knows, your husband he is with us in time for the birthday boy's party, eh?"

They looked at Jay, his mother smiling bravely, and dark-eyed Lena sucking her teeth appraisingly; Jay wanted both women to admire him and also to disappear.

———

When Jay got into bed that night, Lena slid her hand over his hip and cradled his butt.

He tried diverting her. "You really think we can get him out by Thursday?"

She was kissing him now, biting his lip and his ear, her breath sour from red wine and tobacco. "No."

He was appalled. "She'll hear."

"Then don't talk."

But Lena was the one who talked, crying out when she climaxed, "Oh, God!" like some ecstatic penitent crossing gravel on her knees. Later, while Lena sipped *acqua frizzante* and belched softly, she suddenly shushed him even though he hadn't made a sound.

"What?"

"She's crying."

Jay heard his mother's sobs and endured a pang.

"Go. Talk to her."

A *vaporetto* chugged slowly past, the sound echoing between the walls. He found his robe and tied the sash, but hesitated.

She hissed, "Go," and when he still hesitated she punched him on the shoulder.

He swung his arm to knock her hand away but hit only air. He crossed the dark room, three steps carpet, two bare wood, carpet again. "Mom?"

There was an embarrassed silence. "Did I wake you?" Though he assured her she hadn't, she apologized anyway. Sitting up, her hunched posture seemed worse than ever, which irritated him because she was supposed to do exercises.

"It'll work out," he said, the words feeling as false as they sounded.

She nodded though, taking her cue as if they were reciting lines.

"The consul will know what to do. This can't be the first time it's ever happened." Even as he said this he realized it must be true.

"Lena seems nice."

He hadn't said much about her in his emails, other than that she'd been a ballet dancer who'd defected. They'd met in the cemetery on *Isola di San Michele*, his favourite place because it was open and treed and had actual earth under your feet, a rarity in Venice, which eased the ache in his ankles from walking the stone streets. She was putting flowers on a grave when he first saw her. It was hot and the cicadas were rattling. He'd made a point of walking past to see the marker, assuming it was her husband's. In fact, it was the ballet impresario Serge Diaghilev. They took the same boat back across the lagoon.

"It's my fault," said Jay's mother in bed.

"That's crazy."

"He didn't want to go on the cruise. I said I was going whether he did or not." They both knew that the threat of her acting independently was the one thing that could always move him. "He was adamant that he was staying onboard the ship when we reached Constanta. But everyone was going, and the tour was free and –" She shrugged.

"Get some sleep," said Jay, miserable.

"He loves you, Jay."

Crushed, he took that information back to bed where Lena was snoring. He and his father had been distant at best. He lay thinking about his father, who had smuggled himself out of Romania at nineteen in the trunk of a Lada, changed his name, eradicated his accent, and obscured his history.

Whenever Jay had tried prying the story of his escape out of him, he became suspicious and even a little angry, as if Jay's interest was unseemly.

————

They were awakened by the phone ringing shortly after eight in the morning.

"Okay, okay," said Lena. "Yes, okay, okay." She handed the receiver to Jay. "Roma."

He sat up. A Mr. Aldon Carter was introducing himself in a voice so serenely self-assured that for an instant Jay was embarrassed at all the commotion they'd caused. Mr. Carter had already spoken to Bucharest. Jay motioned to his mother, who was peering over the Japanese screen. She approached, clutching the throat of her robe, and put her head next to his.

"We hear about these cases every few months," he was saying. "The Russians and Bulgarians are generally the worst. It's the port officials. They're used to their little fiefdoms, especially in the Black Sea region. Was he not warned of this by the cruise agent?"

Jay's mother shook her head, her skull rolling against his, a disturbingly intimate experience. "No."

"The country code for Romania is forty, four zero. And the city code for Constanta is sixteen, then it's 539 5566. That's the port authority. Try the number then sit tight. All right, looks like I've got a call coming through from Bucharest now. We'll talk shortly."

"All right," said Jay. "Thanks."

But Mr. Carston had already switched lines.

Jay and his mother watched Lena punch the numbers while she practised toe positions on the bare wood. Suddenly she held the pose, toe extended with deer-like poise, and rattled something off in Romanian, which sounded like a combination of Italian and French. Her posture and manner and even her face itself completely transformed when she switched languages. She covered the receiver. "They're transferring me to hotel."

"He's in a hotel?"

Jay's mother, suddenly a ballet dancer herself, pirouetted and threw her arms around him in relief. Jay held his breath.

Lena was speaking Romanian again, and had resumed her toe-step exercises. Suddenly she thrust the phone at Jay's mother.

"Paul? Oh God, it's you!" She was weeping.

Jay leaned close, but his mother's sobs made it frustratingly hard to hear.

"So it's a hotel," his mother was saying. "A *TV*?" She looked at Jay and Lena and, as if it was all turning out to be a lark, said, "He watched Romanian TV last night. So the consul . . . And they're . . . When? Okay, okay . . ." They spoke a few more minutes and his mother was laughing by the time she returned the phone to Lena. "He's talked to the embassy twice and they're arranging a flight. He should be in Rome tomorrow. He'll catch a train."

Lena looked impressed but skeptical. "You look ten years younger."

"I feel it."

"And the money," asked Jay. "The taxes?"

"Paperwork, a mix-up."

"Bravo," said Lena.

The weight of the crisis lifted and Jay's shoulders floated with relief.

To celebrate they breakfasted in a café opposite the Rialto fruit market, where the scent of coffee complemented the smells of Sicilian oranges and Egyptian melons.

"You can see the canal through the arches," Lena pointed out.

Jay's mother admired the sixteenth-century façades reflected in the water. "I can see why you live here."

A sudden downpour forced people to take refuge in the cafés and *loggias*. The happy trio had another coffee and watched the rain bounce like glass beads on the flagstones and set the brown canal boiling.

"TV," she said, laughing, as if the very notion of Romanian TV was absurd.

"What did he watch?" inquired Lena, chin on her palm, gazing at Jay's mother.

"He didn't say."

Jay tried imagining Romanian TV. Italian TV was dominated by soap operas, game shows, and fortune tellers. On any given evening up to four stations featured charlatans loudly dispensing advice on sex and money. Jay's guilty pleasure was the half hour of dubbed Bugs Bunny cartoons each afternoon at five. It occurred to him now that his father had always liked Bugs Bunny as well, that in fact the two of them had often watched together, his dad shaking with suppressed laughter.

The rain passed as suddenly as it started. They crossed the Rialto Bridge and spent the morning admiring the Titians in Santa Maria Gloriosa dei Frari in San Polo, and listening to his mother, suddenly chatty, describe their cruise. The Turks had been hospitable, though they were both constipated from too much bread. They went to a Greek Orthodox monastery near Trebizond where the eyes were gouged out of the frescos. Sevastopol was dusty and people queued for water. In Odessa Jay's father had diarrhea and cramps.

They had lunch at the nearby Trattoria alla Madonna, deciding to save Florian's for when Jay's dad arrived tomorrow. After lunch Lena went off to teach a dance class. The euphoria of relief had ebbed and his mother admitted she could use a nap. The rain had resumed, and on the walk back to the apartment she remarked how crowded and damp the city was.

———

That evening, Jay taught two English classes then wandered over to the *Fondamente Nuove* and stared across the water toward *San Michele*. In ten years he'd be fifty and Lena seventy. Some of the other teachers in the school were older than he was and yet had women in their twenties.

———

Lena phoned the hotel in Constanta the next morning and was told that the police had taken Jay's father to a Bucharest hospital. His mother collapsed. It was as if she'd dissolved inside her clothes, leaving only a puddle of cloth. Jay held her while Lena dialled Mr. Carter in Rome. The line was busy. They tried the embassies in Bucharest and Rome and Ottawa with no luck.

His mother recovered enough to spend the afternoon twisting her fingers as if trying to unscrew them from her knuckles.

They called the cruise line but the ship had left and the head office in Oslo kept them on hold.

Mr. Carter called that night to say that Jay's father was in the hospital of the Bucharest State Prison. "He underwent emergency surgery for a double hernia and is now resting comfortably."

"*Hernia?* You talked to him?" asked Jay.

"To the surgeon."

Jay looked at his mother's wide wet eyes. "But the taxes. That's all cleared up, right?"

Carter's tone became gravely professional. "Two hundred and six thousand dollars. Usually you can make a settlement," he said as if this was all quite normal. "Around twenty-five percent."

"Fifty thousand dollars?"

"I suggest you contact your bank."

Jay, defeated, stared at the faded Turkish rug beneath his feet with its onion domes, tulips, and twining vines.

Later that night he woke and found his mother packing her suitcase.

"Someone has to be there with him."

———

The arrival lounge of the Bucharest airport smelled of damp masonry, the walls were the colour of dried egg yolk, while faulty track lighting spattered sparks on the passengers so that they waved their arms about their heads as if shooing insects. A bored customs agent, with a dangling tie and his hat shoved to the back of his head, ground his stamp into Jay's passport as if crushing a cockroach.

Jay was ashamed at how his resistance had ebbed when his mother bought him a first-class plane ticket and gave him a thousand U.S. dollars. Looking out the window of the plane en route to Bucharest, he'd become emotional at seeing the curve of the earth and remembering that the world extended far beyond Venice's enclosed alleys. The light in the plane had been radiant and he'd wanted to just keep on going.

The prison hospital smelled of disinfectant and the linoleum was spongy under his heels. It was three in the afternoon. He found his father asleep in a narrow bed of grey-painted metal. There was a magazine on the side table folded open to an article on *futbal*. His father knew nothing of *futbal*. He was grey-haired and portly, read historical novels and wore thick glasses. Now he lay unshaved under a yellowed sheet. Had he ever seen his father sleep? He looked like a stranger. Men coughed and talked in low voices with women in scarves and overcoats. A clipboard hung by a wire at the end of the bed and on it was a report typed in faded ink. Jay read the name Bogza, Pavel. The key had punched a hole right through the *o* in *Bogza*. He wanted to weep.

The nurse arrived wearing a smock and what looked like a welder's cap on her flattened blonde hair. Pushing a metal trolley with a loudly wobbling wheel, she worked her way along the row of beds, smoothing blankets and doling out paper cups of medicine. When she reached Jay, she nodded and said something in Romanian. She placed her hand on his dad's shoulder and let the weight of it wake him. Jay thought she was rather attractive in a sturdy fashion, about his age, a little younger. His dad opened his eyes. The nurse was speaking, but his dad didn't hear because he'd spotted him. Without thinking, Jay leaned down and embraced him.

"Your mother –"

"Venice."

He sank back in relief.

The nurse was speaking again but Jay's dad ignored her. "My glasses?"

Jay got his glasses from the side table and this calmed him immediately. "You should leave. There's nothing you can do."

"I came to get you out."

This amused him. In his father's eyes he would always be five years old. "Get yourself out."

The nurse, speaking the entire time, was growing frustrated.

His father looked at her and shrugged. "English," he said. "English." Jay shook his head at the nurse meaning he didn't understand, meaning *neither of them* understood. The nurse was becoming less attractive by the moment as she whined in a thin high voice and rapped the clipboard with her knuckle.

"Please," said Jay, gently taking the clipboard from her reluctant fingers. Her nametag said Sonja. He blacked out the words *Bogza, Pavel*. Speaking the name aloud as he wrote it, he said, "Bond, Paul," and underlined it twice.

————

A day later they were in Venice. His father had had to sign various forms before being allowed on the plane. During the flight he drank Scotch and became morose at his homeland having waited like a spider and finally getting him.

By the time they reached Venice and caught the *vaporetto*, his father was exhausted and sat with his hands like two dead animals in his lap, small old hands that had once held his. The boat churned the water wrinkling the reflections of the Grand Canal's façade, and Jay felt the suffocating city closing in.

"So you're turning forty," his father suddenly stated. He was about to go on, as if there were things he'd been meaning to say, and that now, given all that had happened, was the right time, but at that moment they neared their stop and he spotted his wife. "There she is." There was an endearing relief in his voice and he sat up taller. "Who's that with her?" For a moment Jay wondered as well. Lena looked exactly as he'd left her, but different, someone from a past life.

———

Jay remained crouched down out of sight until the next stop. He looked back, but by then it was too far to see Lena and his parents. He faced forward, propped his elbow on the ledge and leaned his brow in his palm and shut his eyes. The boat pulled in and out of its stops and he remained where he was, listening to the water sluicing past and the people crowding off and on. His father had stared at him for only a few seconds when he'd announced he wasn't going with him, that he was leaving Venice. He read the expression in his son's eyes. He even smiled a little and then nodded as if it was okay, as if he understood, and in that moment Jay had no doubt that he did. They shook hands, the quick firm handshake of comrades, and Jay ducked down as his father disembarked. He could probably have asked his dad anything then, about the escape in the trunk of the Lada, the driver, everything, and got all the details, but that would have to wait for the next time they met.

Andrew J. Borkowski's short fiction has appeared in *The New Quarterly*, *Storyteller*, and *Grain Magazine*, where "Twelve Versions of Lech" was first published. The story is drawn from a collection-in-progress entitled *Copernicus Avenue*, inspired by his early years living in Toronto's Polish community along Roncesvalles Avenue. He has worked as a freelance editor and arts-and-entertainment writer for more than twenty years, with articles appearing in *TV Guide*, *Chatelaine*, *Books in Canada*, *Fashion Magazine*, and *The Canadian Forum*.

Craig Boyko's short fiction has appeared in *filling Station*, *Queen's Quarterly*, *The Malahat Review*, *The New Quarterly*, *Descant*, *Grain Magazine*, and *PRISM international*. Three of his stories have been anthologized in earlier volumes of *The Journey Prize Stories*. His first collection of stories, *Blackouts*, will be published in spring 2008. Born in Saskatchewan, he lived in Calgary for several years before moving to Victoria, British Columbia.

Grant Buday's most recent novel, *Rootbound*, was published by ECW Press. His other novels include *A Sack of Teeth* (Raincoast Books, 2002) and *White Lung* (Anvil Press, 1999). He has two new novels, *The Water Clock*, set on the South

Pacific atoll of Panoah, and *The Horse*, about the Greek hero Odysseus.

After a decade in Toronto, **Nicole Dixon** moved to a lobster-fishing village on the Bay of Fundy in Nova Scotia. In 2005, she won the Bronwen Wallace Memorial Award and was shortlisted for a CBC Literary Award. She holds a Master of Arts in Creative Writing and English from the University of Windsor and was featured on the cover of *The New Quarterly*. She is currently at work on a collection of short stories and teaches online. Please visit nicoledixon.ca

Krista Foss is a fiction writer, journalist, and college instructor who lives in Hamilton, Ontario. "Swimming in Zanzibar" was her first published piece of fiction when it appeared in *The Antigonish Review*. Her non-fiction work has been twice nominated for a National Magazine Award. She is currently at work on a novel and several short stories.

Pasha Malla was born in St. John's, Newfoundland, and probably lives in Toronto. A collection of his stories will be published by House of Anansi Press in 2008, somehow, and in the near future there will likely be a novel.

Alice Petersen grew up in New Zealand. She holds degrees in English Literature from the University of Otago and Queen's

University. Her short fiction has been published in *Tahake*, *Geist*, and in the anthology *Short Stuff: New English Writing in Quebec* (Véhicule Press, 2005). She lives in Montreal, where she is developing a collection of short stories under the guidance of Sandra Birdsell through the Humber School for Writers.

Patricia Robertson is the author of the short story collections *City of Orphans*, which was shortlisted for the Ethel Wilson Fiction Prize, and *The Goldfish Dancer*, which was released in spring 2007. Two of her stories – including "My Hungarian Sister" – have been nominated, in successive years, for a National Magazine Award. A poet and dramatist as well as a fiction writer, Robertson holds a Master of Arts in Creative Writing from Boston University. She lives in Whitehorse, Yukon, where she is at work on two novels and more short stories.

Rebecca Rosenblum completed her Master of Arts in English and Creative Writing at the University of Toronto in 2007. "Chilly Girl," her first published story, appeared in *Exile: The Literary Quarterly*. Since then, her work has appeared in *echolocation*, *The Danforth Review*, *Hart House Review*, *The New Quarterly*, and *Qwerty*. Her first collection of stories will be published by Biblioasis in 2008.

Nicholas Ruddock practises medicine in Guelph, Ontario. He has also lived in Newfoundland and Labrador, the Yukon, and Quebec. In the past two years, he has won the inaugural Sheldon Curry Fiction Prize from *The Antigonish Review* and *Grain Magazine*'s Postcard Story Contest, placed second in *PRISM international*'s Fiction Contest, and has had short fiction published in *The Fiddlehead* and *The Dalhousie Review*. He's tying his stories together into a novel entitled *How Loveta Got Her Baby*.

Jean Van Loon's fiction has appeared in *The Dalhousie Review*, *The New Quarterly*, *Queen's Quarterly*, and *Ottawa Magazine*'s summer fiction issue. She is presently seeking a publisher for her first collection of stories. Before falling in love with fiction, she wrote policy papers, speeches, and briefings as a senior public servant and, later, as President of the Canadian Steel Producers Association. She is a life-long resident of Ottawa.

ABOUT THE CONTRIBUTING JOURNALS

For more information about all the journals that submitted stories to this year's anthology, please consult *The Journey Prize Stories* website: www.mcclelland.com/jps

The Antigonish Review is a creative literary quarterly that publishes poetry, fiction, critical articles, and reviews. We consider stories, poetry, and essays from anywhere – original or in translation – but our mandate is to encourage and publish new and emerging Canadian writers, with special consideration for writers from the Atlantic region who might otherwise go unrecognized. Submissions and correspondence: *The Antigonish Review*, P.O. Box 5000, St. Francis Xavier University, Antigonish, Nova Scotia, B2G 2W5. Website: www.antigonishreview.com

Exile: The Literary Quarterly is a distinctive journal that recently published its Anniversary Special 30 Volumes/120th Issue, featuring new work from, among others, writers who appeared in the first issues (Margaret Atwood and Marie-Claire Blais), the middle issues (Austin Clarke and Susan Swan), and those who continue to carry on the tradition (Priscila Uppal, a finalist for the 2007 Griffin Poetry Prize, and Matt Shaw, winner of the 2005 Journey Prize). With more than one thousand contributions since 1972, *Exile* has become a respected forum, always presenting an impressive selection of new and established authors and artists, drawing our content (literature, poetry, drama, works in translation, and the fine arts) from French and English Canada, as well as from the United States, Britain, Europe, Latin America, the Middle East, and Asia. Publisher: Michael Callaghan. Submissions and correspondence: *Exile*/Excelsior Publishing Inc., 134 Eastbourne Avenue, Toronto, Ontario, M5P 2G6. Email (queries only): exq@exilequarterly.com Website: www.ExileQuarterly.com

The Fiddlehead, Atlantic Canada's longest-running literary journal, publishes poetry and short fiction as well as book reviews. It appears four times a year, sponsors a contest for poetry and fiction that awards a total of $4,000 in prizes, including the $1,000 Ralph Gustafson Poetry Prize. *The Fiddlehead* welcomes all good writing in English, from anywhere, looking always for that element of freshness and surprise. Editor: Ross Leckie. Managing Editor: Kathryn Taglia. Submissions and correspondence: *The Fiddlehead*, Campus House, 11 Garland Court, University of New Brunswick, P.O. Box 4400, Fredericton, New Brunswick, E3B 5A3. Email (queries only): fiddlehd@unb.ca Website: www.lib.unb.ca/Texts/Fiddlehead

Geist is a Canadian magazine of ideas and culture, with a strong literary focus, a special interest in photography, and a sense of humour. The *Geist* tone is intelligent, plain-talking, inclusive, and offbeat. Each issue is a strangely convergent collection of fiction, non-fiction, photographs, comix, reviews, little-known facts of interest, a bit of poetry, and the legendary *Geist* map and crossword puzzle, all of which explore the lines between fiction and non-fiction, and which take a new look at Canada, the country we are all still in the process of imagining. Editor: Stephen Osborne. Submissions and correspondence: *Geist*, #200 – 341 Water Street, Vancouver, British Columbia, V6B 1B8. Email: geist@geist.com Website: www.geist.com

Grain Magazine provides readers with fine, fresh writing by new and established writers of poetry and prose four times a year. Published by the Saskatchewan Writers Guild, *Grain* has earned national and international recognition for its distinctive literary content. Editor: Kent Bruyneel. Fiction Editor: David Carpenter. Poetry Editor: Gerald Hill. Submissions and correspondence: *Grain Magazine*, P.O. Box 67, Saskatoon, Saskatchewan, S7K 3K1. Email: grainmag@sasktel.net Website: www.grainmagazine.ca

Maisonneuve Magazine is a bimonthly magazine based in Montreal and published in English, which aims to keep its readers informed, alert, and entertained. *Maisonneuve* was recently awarded the prestigious President's Medal at the Twenty-Eighth Annual National Magazine Awards for best overall editorial achievement of the year. *Maisonneuve* has been described as "the magazine for people who give a damn." Editor-in-Chief: Derek Webster. Managing Editor: Meredith Erickson. Submissions and correspondence: *Maisonneuve Magazine*, 400 de Maisonneuve West, Suite 655, Montreal, Quebec, H3A 1L4. Email: submissions@maisonneuve.org Website: www.maisonneuve.org

The Malahat Review, now in its fortieth year, is a quarterly journal of contemporary poetry and fiction by both new and celebrated writers. Summer issues feature the winners of *Malahat*'s Novella and Long Poem prizes, held in alternate years; the Fall issues feature the winners of the Far Horizons Award for emerging writers, alternating poetry and fiction each year; the Winter issues feature the winners of the Creative Non-Fiction Prize. All issues feature covers by noted Canadian visual artists and include reviews of Canadian books. Editor: John Barton. Assistant Editor: Rhonda Batchelor. Submissions and correspondence: *The Malahat Review*, University of Victoria, P.O. Box 1700, Station CSC, Victoria, British Columbia, V8W 2Y2. Email: malahat@uvic.ca Website: www.malahatreview.ca

The New Quarterly is an award-winning literary magazine publishing fiction, poetry, interviews, and essays on writing. Now in its twenty-sixth year, the magazine prides itself on its independent take on the Canadian literary scene. Recent issues have been devoted to comedy, genre writing, and occasional verse. Best known for our fiction, we also publish a series on the intersection of word and image and on the seductions of verse. Editor: Kim Jernigan. Submissions and correspondence: *The New Quarterly*, c/o St. Jerome's University, 290 Westmount Road North, Waterloo, Ontario, N2L 3G3. Email: editor@tnq.ca Website: www.tnq.ca

PRISM international, the oldest literary magazine in Western Canada, was established in 1959 by a group of

Vancouver writers. Published four times a year, *PRISM* features short fiction, poetry, drama, creative non-fiction, and translations by both new and established writers from Canada and around the world. The only criteria are originality and quality. *PRISM* holds three exemplary competitions: the Short Fiction Contest, the Literary Non-fiction Contest, and the Earle Birney Prize for Poetry. Executive Editors: Kellee Ngan and Jamella Hagen. Fiction Editor: Claire Tacon. Poetry Editor: Sheryda Warrener. Submissions and correspondence: *PRISM international*, Creative Writing Program, The University of British Columbia, Buchanan E-462, 1866 Main Mall, Vancouver, British Columbia, V6T 1Z1. Email (for queries only): prism@interchange.ubc.ca Website: www.prism.arts.ubc.ca

Queen's Quarterly, founded in 1893, is the oldest intellectual journal in Canada. It publishes articles on a variety of subjects and consequently fiction occupies relatively little space. There are one or two stories in each issue. However, because of its lively format and eclectic mix of subject matter, *Queen's Quarterly* attracts readers with widely diverse interests. This exposure is an advantage many of our fiction writers appreciate. Submissions are welcome from both new and established writers. Fiction Editor: Joan Harcourt. Submissions and correspondence: *Queen's Quarterly*, Queen's University, 144 Barrie Street, Kingston, Ontario, K7L 3N6. Email: qquarter@queensu.ca Website: www.queensu.ca/ quarterly

Submissions were also received from the following journals:

Broken Pencil
(Toronto, Ont.)

The Capilano Review
(North Vancouver, B.C.)

The Claremont Review
(Victoria, B.C.)

The Dalhousie Review
(Halifax, N.S.)

Descant
(Toronto, Ont.)

Event
(New Westminster, B.C.)

Kiss Machine
(Toronto, Ont.)

LICHEN Arts & Letters Preview
(Whitby, Ont.)

Matrix Magazine
(Montreal, Que.)

The New Orphic Review
(Nelson, B.C.)

Prairie Fire
(Winnipeg, Man.)

Prairie Journal
(Calgary, Alta.)

Room of One's Own
(Vancouver, B.C.)

Storyteller
(Ottawa, Ont.)

sub-TERRAIN Magazine
(Vancouver, B.C.)

Taddle Creek
(Toronto, Ont.)

This Magazine
(Toronto, Ont.)

Windsor Review
(Windsor, Ont.)

PREVIOUS CONTRIBUTING AUTHORS

* Winners of the $10,000 Journey Prize
** Co-winners of the $10,000 Journey Prize

I

1989

SELECTED WITH ALISTAIR MacLEOD

Ven Bègamudré, "Word Games"

David Bergen, "Where You're From"

Lois Braun, "The Pumpkin-Eaters"

Constance Buchanan, "Man with Flying Genitals"

Ann Copeland, "Obedience"

Marion Douglas, "Flags"

Frances Itani, "An Evening in the Café"

Diane Keating, "The Crying Out"

Thomas King, "One Good Story, That One"

Holley Rubinsky, "Rapid Transits"*

Jean Rysstad, "Winter Baby"

Kevin Van Tighem, "Whoopers"

M.G. Vassanji, "In the Quiet of a Sunday Afternoon"

Bronwen Wallace, "Chicken 'N' Ribs"

Armin Wiebe, "Mouse Lake"

Budge Wilson, "Waiting"

2

1990

SELECTED WITH LEON ROOKE; GUY VANDERHAEGHE

André Alexis, "Despair: Five Stories of Ottawa"

Glen Allen, "The Hua Guofeng Memorial Warehouse"

Marusia Bociurkiw, "Mama, Donya"

Virgil Burnett, "Billfrith the Dreamer"

Margaret Dyment, "Sacred Trust"

Cynthia Flood, "My Father Took a Cake to France"*

Douglas Glover, "Story Carved in Stone"

Terry Griggs, "Man with the Axe"

Rick Hillis, "Limbo River"

Thomas King, "The Dog I Wish I Had, I Would Call It Helen"

K.D. Miller, "Sunrise Till Dark"

Jennifer Mitton, "Let Them Say"

Lawrence O'Toole, "Goin' to Town with Katie Ann"

Kenneth Radu, "A Change of Heart"

Jenifer Sutherland, "Table Talk"

Wayne Tefs, "Red Rock and After"

3

1991

SELECTED WITH JANE URQUHART

Donald Aker, "The Invitation"

Anton Baer, "Yukon"

Allan Barr, "A Visit from Lloyd"

David Bergen, "The Fall"

Rai Berzins, "Common Sense"

Diana Hartog, "Theories of Grief"

Diane Keating, "The Salem Letters"

Yann Martel, "The Facts Behind the Helsinki Roccamatios"*
Jennifer Mitton, "Polaroid"
Sheldon Oberman, "This Business with Elijah"
Lynn Podgurny, "Till Tomorrow, Maple Leaf Mills"
James Riseborough, "She Is Not His Mother"
Patricia Stone, "Living on the Lake"

4

1992

SELECTED WITH SANDRA BIRDSELL

David Bergen, "The Bottom of the Glass"
Maria A. Billion, "No Miracles Sweet Jesus"
Judith Cowan, "By the Big River"
Steven Heighton, "A Man Away from Home Has No Neighbours"
Steven Heighton, "How Beautiful upon the Mountains"
L. Rex Kay, "Travelling"
Rozena Maart, "No Rosa, No District Six"*
Guy Malet De Carteret, "Rainy Day"
Carmelita McGrath, "Silence"
Michael Mirolla, "A Theory of Discontinuous Existence"
Diane Juttner Perreault, "Bella's Story"
Eden Robinson, "Traplines"

5

1993

SELECTED WITH GUY VANDERHAEGHE

Caroline Adderson, "Oil and Dread"
David Bergen, "La Rue Prevette"
Marina Endicott, "With the Band"
Dayv James-French, "Cervine"

Michael Kenyon, "Durable Tumblers"

K.D. Miller, "A Litany in Time of Plague"

Robert Mullen, "Flotsam"

Gayla Reid, "Sister Doyle's Men"*

Oakland Ross, "Bang-bang"

Robert Sherrin, "Technical Battle for Trial Machine"

Carol Windley, "The Etruscans"

6

1994

SELECTED WITH DOUGLAS GLOVER;
JUDITH CHANT (CHAPTERS)

Anne Carson, "Water Margins: An Essay on Swimming by My Brother"

Richard Cumyn, "The Sound He Made"

Genni Gunn, "Versions"

Melissa Hardy, "Long Man the River"*

Robert Mullen, "Anomie"

Vivian Payne, "Free Falls"

Jim Reil, "Dry"

Robyn Sarah, "Accept My Story"

Joan Skogan, "Landfall"

Dorothy Speak, "Relatives in Florida"

Alison Wearing, "Notes from Under Water"

7

1995

SELECTED WITH M.G. VASSANJI;

RICHARD BACHMANN (A DIFFERENT DRUMMER BOOKS)

Michelle Alfano, "Opera"

Mary Borsky, "Maps of the Known World"

Gabriella Goliger, "Song of Ascent"

Elizabeth Hay, "Hand Games"

Shaena Lambert, "The Falling Woman"

Elise Levine, "Boy"

Roger Burford Mason, "The Rat-Catcher's Kiss"

Antanas Sileika, "Going Native"

Kathryn Woodward, "Of Marranos and Gilded Angels"*

8

1996

SELECTED WITH OLIVE SENIOR;

BEN MCNALLY (NICHOLAS HOARE LTD.)

Rick Bowers, "Dental Bytes"

David Elias, "How I Crossed Over"

Elyse Gasco, "Can You Wave Bye Bye, Baby?"*

Danuta Gleed, "Bones"

Elizabeth Hay, "The Friend"

Linda Holeman, "Turning the Worm"

Elaine Littman, "The Winner's Circle"

Murray Logan, "Steam"

Rick Maddocks, "Lessons from the Sputnik Diner"

K.D. Miller, "Egypt Land"

Gregor Robinson, "Monster Gaps"

Alma Subasic, "Dust"

9

1997

SELECTED WITH NINO RICCI;

NICHOLAS PASHLEY (UNIVERSITY OF TORONTO BOOKSTORE)

Brian Bartlett, "Thomas, Naked"

Dennis Bock, "Olympia"

Kristen den Hartog, "Wave"

Gabriella Goliger, "Maladies of the Inner Ear"**

Terry Griggs, "Momma Had a Baby"

Mark Anthony Jarman, "Righteous Speedboat"

Judith Kalman, "Not for Me a Crown of Thorns"

Andrew Mullins, "The World of Science"

Sasenarine Persaud, "Canada Geese and Apple Chatney"

Anne Simpson, "Dreaming Snow"**

Sarah Withrow, "Ollie"

Terence Young, "The Berlin Wall"

10

1998

SELECTED BY PETER BUITENHUIS, HOLLEY RUBINSKY;

CELIA DUTHIE (DUTHIE BOOKS LTD.)

John Brooke, "The Finer Points of Apples"*

Ian Colford, "The Reason for the Dream"

Libby Creelman, "Cruelty"

Michael Crummey, "Serendipity"

Stephen Guppy, "Downwind"

Jane Eaton Hamilton, "Graduation"

Elise Levine, "You Are You Because Your Little Dog Loves You"

Jean McNeil, "Bethlehem"

Liz Moore, "Eight-Day Clock"

Edward O'Connor, "The Beatrice of Victoria College"

Tim Rogers, "Scars and Other Presents"

Denise Ryan, "Marginals, Vivisections, and Dreams"

Madeleine Thien, "Simple Recipes"

Cheryl Tibbetts, "Flowers of Africville"

11

1999

SELECTED BY LESLEY CHOYCE; SHELDON CURRIE;

MARY-JO ANDERSON (FROG HOLLOW BOOKS)

Mike Barnes, "In Florida"

Libby Creelman, "Sunken Island"

Mike Finigan, "Passion Sunday"

Jane Eaton Hamilton, "Territory"

Mark Anthony Jarman, "Travels into Several Remote Nations of
the World"

Barbara Lambert, "Where the Bodies Are Kept"

Linda Little, "The Still"

Larry Lynch, "The Sitter"

Sandra Sabatini, "The One With the News"

Sharon Steams, "Brothers"

Mary Walters, "Show Jumping"

Alissa York, "The Back of the Bear's Mouth"*

12

2000

SELECTED BY CATHERINE BUSH; HAL NIEDZVIECKI;

MARC GLASSMAN (PAGES BOOKS AND MAGAZINES)

Andrew Gray, "The Heart of the Land"

Lee Henderson, "Sheep Dub"

Jessica Johnson, "We Move Slowly"

John Lavery, "The Premier's New Pyjamas"

J.A. McCormack, "Hearsay"

Nancy Richler, "Your Mouth Is Lovely"

Andrew Smith, "Sightseeing"

Karen Solie, "Onion Calendar"

Timothy Taylor, "Doves of Townsend"*

Timothy Taylor, "Pope's Own"

Timothy Taylor, "Silent Cruise"

R.M. Vaughan, "Swan Street"

13

2001

SELECTED BY ELYSE GASCO; MICHAEL HELM;

MICHAEL NICHOLSON (INDIGO BOOKS & MUSIC INC.)

Kevin Armstrong, "The Cane Field"*

Mike Barnes, "Karaoke Mon Amour"

Heather Birrell, "Machaya"

Heather Birrell, "The Present Perfect"

Craig Boyko, "The Gun"

Vivette J. Kady, "Anything That Wiggles"

Billie Livingston, "You're Taking All the Fun Out of It"

Annabel Lyon, "Fishes"

Lisa Moore, "The Way the Light Is"

Heather O'Neill, "Little Suitcase"

Susan Rendell, "In the Chambers of the Sea"

Tim Rogers, "Watch"

Margrith Schraner, "Dream Dig"

14

2002

SELECTED BY ANDRÉ ALEXIS;

DEREK McCORMACK; DIANE SCHOEMPERLEN

Mike Barnes, "Cogagwee"

Geoffrey Brown, "Listen"

Jocelyn Brown, "Miss Canada"*

Emma Donoghue, "What Remains"

Jonathan Goldstein, "You Are a Spaceman With Your Head Under the Bathroom Stall Door"

Robert McGill, "Confidence Men"

Robert McGill, "The Stars Are Falling"

Nick Melling, "Philemon"

Robert Mullen, "Alex the God"

Karen Munro, "The Pool"

Leah Postman, "Being Famous"

Neil Smith, "Green Fluorescent Protein"

15

2003

SELECTED BY MICHELLE BERRY;

TIMOTHY TAYLOR; MICHAEL WINTER

Rosaria Campbell, "Reaching"

Hilary Dean, "The Lemon Stories"

Dawn Rae Downton, "Hansel and Gretel"

Anne Fleming, "Gay Dwarves of America"

Elyse Friedman, "Truth"

Charlotte Gill, "Hush"

Jessica Grant, "My Husband's Jump"*

Jacqueline Honnet, "Conversion Classes"

S.K. Johannesen, "Resurrection"

Avner Mandelman, "Cuckoo"

Tim Mitchell, "Night Finds Us"

Heather O'Neill, "The Difference Between Me and Goldstein"

16

2004

SELECTED BY ELIZABETH HAY;

LISA MOORE, MICHAEL REDHILL

Anar Ali, "Baby Khaki's Wings"

Kenneth Bonert, "Packers and Movers"

Jennifer Clouter, "Benny and the Jets"

Daniel Griffin, "Mercedes Buyer's Guide"

Michael Kissinger, "Invest in the North"

Devin Krukoff, "The Last Spark"*

Elaine McCluskey, "The Watermelon Social"

William Metcalfe, "Nice Big Car, Rap Music Coming Out the
Window"

Lesley Millard, "The Uses of the Neckerchief"

Adam Lewis Schroeder, "Burning the Cattle at Both Ends"

Michael V. Smith, "What We Wanted"

Neil Smith, "Isolettes"

Patricia Rose Young, "Up the Clyde on a Bike"

17

2005

SELECTED BY JAMES GRAINGER AND NANCY LEE

Randy Boyagoda, "Rice and Curry Yacht Club"

Krista Bridge, "A Matter of Firsts"

Josh Byer, "Rats, Homosex, Saunas, and Simon"

Craig Davidson, "Failure to Thrive"

McKinley M. Hellenes, "Brighter Thread"

Catherine Kidd, "Green-Eyed Beans"

Pasha Malla, "The Past Composed"

Edward O'Connor, "Heard Melodies Are Sweet"

Barbara Romanik, "Seven Ways into Chandigarh"

Sandra Sabatini, "The Dolphins at Sainte Marie"

Matt Shaw, "Matchbook for a Mother's Hair"*

Richard Simas, "Anthropologies"

Neil Smith, "Scrapbook"

Emily White, "Various Metals"

18

2006

SELECTED BY STEVEN GALLOWAY;

ZSUZSI GARTNER; ANNABEL LYON

Heather Birrell, "BriannaSusannaAlana"*

Craig Boyko, "The Baby"

Craig Boyko, "The Beloved Departed"

Nadia Bozak, "Heavy Metal Housekeeping"

Lee Henderson, "Conjugation"

Melanie Little, "Wrestling"

Matthew Rader, "The Lonesome Death of Joseph Fey"

Scott Randall, "Law School"
Sarah Selecky, "Throwing Cotton"
Damian Tarnopolsky, "Sleepy"
Martin West, "Cretacea"
David Whitton, "The Eclipse"
Clea Young, "Split"